The Ghost and Me, Joey

IRIS M. DRZEWIECKI

H·H

Hull House

CIRCA 1810

Western New York Heritage Press, Inc.
Cheektowaga, New York

WESTERN NEW YORK
Heritage
Press, Inc.

Western New York Heritage Press, Inc.

495 Pine Ridge Heritage Blvd.

Cheektowaga, New York 14225-2503

Design of Logo & Floor Plans © 2002 by Daniel Drzewiecki
Illustrations & Cover © 2002 by Roger Leyonmark

ISBN 1-878097-21-0

1. Frontier and Pioneer Life – Fiction 2. Ghosts – Fiction
I. Title

This book is a work of fiction. Although certain historical figures,
events, and locales are portrayed, they are used fictitiously.
Any resemblance to persons living or dead is purely coincidental.

Printed in United States of America

Dedicated to my husband Dan,

for his support and encouragement,

And to my grandchildren,

who were my inspiration.

FOREWORD

The old stone house built by Revolutionary War veteran Warren Hull really exists. It has been vacant for over fifteen years. As a historian, I have given tours of the house and have seen first-hand how young people are immediately attracted by it. The house fires their imagination and transports them back in time to the very beginnings of our country. From the pioneer basement kitchen to the timeless timber attic, the house enables them to peer through layers of history.

The Warren Hull house stands like a silent grey sentinel guarding its own history. For almost two hundred years, it has survived on its own without any special outside protection. It almost seems as though it weathered the years under the protection of some special providence, some kind spirit watching over it.

Grownups, too, can sense the spirit of the house. Iris Drzewiecki, the author, is one of those who have come under its benign spell. This story is the result of that attraction. Iris has a special gift for seeing through the eyes of Joey, putting it into words, and making the house and its history come alive through Joey's imagination.

John H. Conlin
October, 2002

CHAPTER 1

The first time I saw the ghost was on a Saturday, the day after my tenth birthday. Dad made me go with him to the old house again because he had to mow the overgrown grass. He worked there a lot because he's Director of the Landmark Society, a group that likes old places and tries to save them from being torn down. Hull House is Dad's favorite because it's the oldest stone homestead in the county. It was built by a Revolutionary War soldier who is buried in the back yard.

Some of the kids at school said the house was haunted by the ghost of Lancaster. It really didn't bother me until Richie (the class bully) started mocking me. He thinks he's tough and knows everything. It's as if he thinks he's the teacher. This really gets on my nerves.

He said, "Joe, I dare you to go up to the attic next time you're there. I'll bet that's where the ghost lives."

I stuck out my chin, looked him straight in the eye and said, "Sure, I'll go up to the attic. Actually, I'd like to see the ghost!" I'd never been up there before, but I didn't want Richie to think I was chicken.

It wasn't long before that boast came back to haunt me because that Saturday, my dad insisted I was going to Hull House with him. I wanted to stay home because I was working on my newest airplane model. It was a birthday gift from Mike, my best friend. Dad kept calling me, telling me to hurry up. Now I could hear his footsteps coming up to my room.

His voice boomed, "Come on, Joey, let's go."

I put another piece on the Tomcat, turned and pleaded, "Really, Dad, I don't want to go to that stupid place again!"

"You have to Joey, since Mom and Andrea went to the mall."

"Can't I stay home alone? Now that I'm ten, I should be able to."

"I said NO and that's final."

I kicked my model box into a corner, complaining, "Shoot! I'm so sick of going to Hull House. It's a waste of time."

Dad said, "Joe, you know it's my dream that someday it will be a museum."

"Yeah, well right now it's a nightmare to me."

"Why don't you bring your new camera along and try it out? You might have some fun taking pictures there."

I guessed that was a good idea. It would keep me from being bored. I grabbed my camera and loaded the film on the drive to the house.

Dad parked the car and smiled. "Why don't you start by photographing the front of the house, Joey?"

Beats me the way he enjoyed being there. The old place looked crooked and crumbly. The roof needed repair; chimney bricks were missing; paint was peeling; stone steps were cracked; porch boards were rotted. It looked really freaky to me. But I took a few outside shots to make him happy.

Dad unlocked the old, creaky front door and said, "I'll be busy outside for about an hour. Look around inside but watch out for loose floor boards."

When I walked in, the cold, clammy air gave me goosebumps. It smelled musty and made me cough. The corners were draped with cobwebs that brushed against my face. As I moved around taking pictures, my sneakers made tracks on the dusty floor. When I finished downstairs, I started up the steep steps to the attic.

Suddenly, Richie's big belly laugh echoed in my head. I remembered him saying, "The ghost house kid thinks he's gutsy. I'd like to see that!"

The old stairs gave a spooky squeak. Although sunbeams floated in the dusty air, a shiver shook my spine. I lifted the old latch and held my breath as the door creaked open. I peered into the shadowy, creepy attic. Its silence sucked me in, like a giant straw.

I talked to myself, hoping the sound would drive away my fear. Well, if I got a couple of pictures up here, I could shove them in Richie's face.

I took pictures from all sides, then noticed the huge beams overhead. To help me balance and aim up, I wedged myself in the corner. The camera flashed and slipped from my hands. I picked it up and hit my head on a low rafter.

"Ouch," I said out loud, "that really hurt!"

I hoped the camera didn't break. I moved closer to the window to check for damage. As I rubbed some of the grime off a pane of glass to get more light, I heard a low grumble.

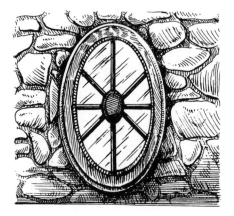

I froze and stared at the window. It seemed to be fogging up and moving. I must have hit my head really hard! I was seeing things.

The swirling settled into the face of an old man. A raspy voice grated, "Ahh, good."

"What? This can't be real!"

"Welcome, young man," murmured the voice.

I wanted to turn and run, but my feet were glued to the floor. I wanted to yell for Dad, but my voice was locked. I thought, get hold of yourself, Joey; this is just an attic. There's no such thing as a ghost. But there he was, right before my eyes!

The ghost smiled, and his overgrown beard whirled under his chin like a billowing cloud. "Do not be frightened, I mean you no harm."

My voice squeaked, "Who—who are you?"

"I am Warren Hull, the builder of this house. I have been watching you and am grateful that you finally released me."

I kept my eyes targeted on him, afraid to look away. His wide brimmed hat covered his long hair, framing a face that made me think of a stone statue, weathered and worn. His clothes covered a large belly that seemed to float.

My knees shook. "Holy cow! Then you are the ghost of Lancaster!"

"By golden, I am. I am always here in my beautiful house, but I can only reveal myself to youngsters who are brave and really want to see me. What is your name, lad?"

"It's Joey. Joey Evans."

I gaped at him, my mind struggling to believe my eyes. Then I got a cold, scary feeling, not bad-scary, but excited-scary, like before I ride down the roller coaster at Darien Lake.

I gulped, "Wow, this is neat. I'm talking to a ghost! Have you been here long?"

"Yes, indeed, since my death in 1838. My spirit cannot rest until I know the house that I built so long ago will stand strong through the ages."

"Oh, my dad and the Landmark Society are trying to preserve it."

"I know. He is a very hardworking man, but he needs the aid of many more. I hope you will help him."

"Me? What can I do? I'm just a kid."

"I am not certain, but perhaps if you learn more about the house, you can find other young people to aid us. I fear that your father's effort will be the last chance to save it from being destroyed."

"Yeah, it's really kind of falling apart."

"Oh, it was a glorious place when it was built in 1810."

"What was it like around here then?"

"Life was rugged, Joseph. The building of this house was hard won. I have many stories to tell about pioneer life. But you must promise never to reveal the secret of my presence, or I will not be able to communicate with you again."

I nodded. "I promise."

Then the ghost's image fluttered and he said, "Hush, do you hear a voice?"

My eyes bugged out as I heard my father call, "I'm through, Joey. Are you ready to leave?"

The specter grew dimmer and his voice trembled, "Farewell. Come back soooon, my lad."

Then he vanished. Part of me wanted to pull him back into the attic, but the rest of me ran down the stairs and out into the sunshine.

Driving back, Dad asked me why I was so quiet. I just shrugged my shoulders, remembering my promise to the ghost. I had to keep his secret.

When we got home, my mother and sister were opening the door. Mom smiled and carried a large pizza box. "We shopped longer than we were supposed to, so, no time to cook tonight!"

Andrea bounced into the house and called, "It's your favorite, Joe, cheese and pepperoni!"

I ate my pizza like a robot, hardly tasting it. My sister was babbling something about shopping, but I didn't care. Then I noticed everyone staring at me. "What?"

Mom said, "You look tired, Joey. Are you okay?"

"Oh yeah, I just have a headache 'cause I banged my head today."

"Is there a bump? Let's have a look at it."

"No, really, I'm fine. What I want to know is, when are you going to the house again, Dad?"

"I planned on going tomorrow, Joey. Why?"

"Well, could I go with you? I'd really like to."

Dad raised his eyebrows and said, "Really? Wow, Joey, that's nice to hear. You never seemed interested before."

"I know, Dad, but since.....er, we're learning about local stuff, I'd like to get more involved. Besides, I want to finish my roll of film."

Mom laughed, "Guess we've got another preservationist in the family, Andrea."

My sister jumped in front of me, howled, and waved her grabby hands in my face. "Yeah, but that house is haunted. You'd better be careful, Joey, that the ghost doesn't catch you."

"Stop bugging me, Andrea. You're a pain! What do you know anyway? An eight-year-old doesn't know anything!" I stomped out of the kitchen and slammed the door. I picked up my ball and began shooting baskets. It always helped me unwind when I felt uptight inside. Each toss seemed to follow a question in my mind:

Did I actually see the ghost? Thunk, bounce, bounce.

Did the ghost ask me to help save Hull House? Thunk, bounce, bounce.

What am I going to do? Thunk, bounce, bounce.

Could I somehow help my dad preserve it? Thunk, bounce, bounce.

Can I keep the secret as I promised? Thunk, bounce, bounce.

I dropped the ball as Mom's voice cut into my rhythm. "Joey, better come in now. You have to practice your trumpet before 'Star Trek' comes on."

My feet carried me into my room, my hands opened my trumpet case, my lips pursed to play, my ears heard the notes blast out, but somehow my mind was disconnected. Even during my favorite TV show, it was hard to focus.

I wished I could get my friends to help. Maybe a team of the smartest kids in my class could come up with ideas. I'd choose Ted, Mike, Molly, Claire, Kristen, Nicole and Emily. But I was in this alone. I had promised not to tell anyone about the ghost.

At bedtime I said, "Remember, Dad, I'm going with you tomorrow!"

He smiled and said, "Sure, glad to have you."

As I drifted off to sleep, I wondered....Do ghosts show up in pictures?

CHAPTER 2

The next day, I gazed at the old house and thought, it doesn't look so spooky. I can do this. I'm not a wimp. "Give me the keys, Dad, and I'll unlock the door."

"Sure, Joe. Have fun but be careful!"

I hurried into the house. Climbing the stairs to the attic made my hands sweat and my heart thump. I rubbed the window pane gently, but deliberately, and held my breath until the ghost appeared.

"Welcome back, my lad!"

"I—I—I," I stuttered, "wasn't sure you were real... ER... I mean really here!"

"By golden, I am! I hoped we could visit again soon."

"I have so many questions for you."

"Good. I shall do my best to answer."

My knees wobbled, so I plunked down on the floor, crossed my legs, and never took my eyes off the ghost.

"What is your first question, Joseph?"

"Well....were you born here?'

"No, I was born in 1762 in Connecticut. When I was 17, I enlisted in the Massachusetts militia and served two years during the Revolutionary War."

"When did you come to Erie county?"

"In 1804 I purchased this land from the Holland Land Company. The forty-mile journey took three days from the Land Office in Batavia to Lancaster."

"Batavia? We go there to visit. It takes about forty-five minutes to drive there on the thruway."

"Sakes alive, Joseph, the world has speeded up! Back then, I drove my wagon pulled by oxen. Behind me, my boys drove our cow, a few sheep and hogs, while my wife and daughters trudged along on foot. They took turns sitting in the wagon a spell. We rested in taverns along the way."

"You must have really needed a place to rest."

"Ay-yup, for much work was ahead. My cousin and I built a log cabin the year before but the forest was still dense and dangerous. We had to be wary of panthers, wolves and bears."

"Panthers and bears?" I gulped. "I didn't know they were here in Lancaster!"

"Oh, indeed. My neighbor spotted a panther slinking about her yard when her children were outside. She grabbed her husband's gun, which was much too heavy for her, rested it on the back of a chair, and aimed out the window. The varmint was killed with that first shot."

"Wow, women had to be brave too!"

"Brave and bold, Joseph. Before this house was built, we lived in a rough log cabin. I recall when I went to Batavia and left my wife alone with our children. One night, she heard a terrible howl. She saw a pack of wolves who were brazen enough to come up to within a few feet of the door opening that was covered with only a blanket. The wolves were probably after the animals in the kitchen shed. Polly did not want to waken the children for fear their voices would agitate the critters, so she found my ax and stood guard until sunrise when the wolves retreated into the forest."

"Were you on the lookout for panthers and wolves all the time?"

"Ay-up, but bears were also a menace. My friend, Philip Peckham, was a great hunter who joined a group of men stalking a big black bear that had caused much damage. Phil dug a huge pit, camouflaged it with branches and leaves, and sent all the other men away. With only a knife for a weapon and a live pig for bait, he waited for three nights until the bear came. There was a terrible battle but he and his pig came out alive! He had the bearskin made into a great coat as proof of his victory."

"Cool, that guy was really brave. Those animals were sure scary."

"Yea, verily, but there were less of them as we cut trees to open the land for crops."

"How much land did you have?"

"I owned 300 acres, mostly behind the house."

"Wow, the Lancaster Speedway is there now."

"Hum, hum, hum, I do not comprehend that term, my lad."

I thought, sure, he wouldn't know about things invented after his death.

The ghost quivered and continued a low humming sound.

I asked, "When did you start to build this house?"

He brightened. "In 1808 I was able to get planks made at the Bowmansville saw mill. It was finally finished when the limestone was applied in 1810."

"Did you build it yourself?"

His voice boomed, "By golden, I did, with the help of my sons and carpenter friends. We must not lose it now!"

"Geez, you really love this place."

The ghost pleaded, "Help us save it, lad, help us."

"I don't know what I can do."

"Muster your courage, Joseph, and you will find a way. Hark! Someone calls!"

Dad yelled, "Joey, where are you? Look who's here."

I jumped to my feet and backed out of the attic as the ghost melted into the window frame. As I ran down the stairs, Dad walked in with my teacher, Mr. Weston.

The tall, thin man grinned. "Hi, Joey! I saw your dad working outside and he invited me in."

"Oh, good," I stammered.

"Everything okay, son?"

"Yeah, Dad, I'm just surprised to see Mr. Weston here."

"I thought you would be."

My teacher looked around. "I've always wanted to see the inside of Hull House."

Dad replied, "You know it was built by a Revolutionary War soldier in 1810."

"Yes. I understand he's buried in the back yard?"

"He and his wife are way out back, covered by myrtle, a common graveyard plant. Unfortunately, the stone marking his wife Polly's grave has been stolen."

"Too bad," mused Ward Weston. "We need to preserve as much of our history as possible."

Dad shook his head. "That's what we're trying to do with the Landmark Society!"

"Which brings me to my real reason for stopping. We're working on a community unit in school. We could benefit from your expertise in history. Would you be willing to be a guest speaker for our class?"

Dad smiled. "I would be pleased to share what I know about this house."

Mr. Weston said, "How do you feel about your father's visit, Joey? Is it okay with you?"

Dad laughed. "I'm afraid Joey might be turned off by this house. I've dragged him here so many times, he's probably bored with all my stories."

"No Dad, really, I think it would be great to tell the other kids about this house!" I remembered the ghost's appeal to get others involved.

The two men shook hands as they walked out the door. My teacher said, "See you in school tomorrow, Joey."

My brain was glutted with ghost thoughts. I was glad to hear Dad say, "Let's lock up and get home!"

At home, I went outside to clear my head and whistled for my dog. Libby is a yellow lab I've had for seven years. We're real buddies. She sleeps in my room at night and lays her head in my lap when I watch TV. Mom says she thinks Libby is "velcroed" to me.

I threw the Frisbee and she raced, leaped and glided down happily after the catch. As she came back panting, I asked her the question bugging me. "What could I possibly do to help save Hull House?"

Libby whimpered as if she understood.

CHAPTER 3

I walked into my classroom on Monday and saw some boys standing around Richie's desk. The creep looked up and mocked, "Hah, here comes the ghost house kid! He's going to tell us all about the ghost of Lancaster."

"NOT," I replied, as I stood up straight and met Richie eye to eye.

"I'll bet you didn't even go up to the attic," Richie said.

"Sure, I did. You can see all the way to Lancaster Speedway from up there. It's great."

Brucie (also known as my shadow) said, "Gee, do you think I could go with you sometime to see the house?"

"Sure, but guess what? Mr. Weston invited my dad to talk to our class about the house. Maybe you can ask him about seeing it."

Richie laughed. "I should go with you, Brucie, to protect you from the ghost."

Richie is a real pain in the butt. I wish I had the power to call the shots instead of him. I could if I had a setup like the one on a neat TV program. It's about a kid my age who keeps a secret video diary on what's happening in his life. He has a whole slew of equipment in his attic and 100 eyeballs hidden all over to spy on people.

It breaks me up when he edits what's happening, like having steam come out of his dad's ears when he's mad. The best episode was when he smeared his sister's face with whiteout so she disappeared. He can rewind a scene and make it come out the way he wants it to end.

I wanted to erase Richie from this scene right now.

The teacher came in and asked everyone to sit down and open their Social Studies books.

Brucie said, "Mr. Weston, I left my book at home. Can I share Joey's book with him?"

"All right, Bruce, but be more careful about bringing books back. You seem to have trouble remembering lately."

Klutzy Bruce stumbled over his own feet, and the class laughed. He was off in space, as usual, and whispered, "Boy, Joey, I wish you'd take me to the old house soon."

"Shut up, Brucie. We can't talk about it now."

The Social Studies chapter explained how the Holland Land Company sold land to the pioneers. My mind kept wandering back to the ghost's stories of the pioneers' bravery in settling the land. I wished I could stand up and tell everyone what he said. It was hard to keep that bubble of a secret from bursting through my thoughts into my voice.

Bruce's nonstop fidgeting was a pain, and I was glad when the lesson ended.

It bugged me even more when Bruce said, "Remember, Joey, I'm going home with you. Parent-teacher conferences are today and my mom called your mom about it."

"Oh—right, I forgot."

"Maybe we can work on your new plane model."

"Sure."

"What's your mom having for lunch?"

"I don't know, Brucie. We'll find out later." I wanted to tell him if he stopped thinking about food so much, he might not be so fat.

Mom greeted us at the door. "Hi, boys. I was just about to start lunch but I wanted to ask Bruce if he'd like a hot dog."

Bruce shrugged his shoulders and mumbled, "Well, I guess so."

"You don't sound very sure, Bruce," said Mom.

"It's because, well, I usually barf after eating hot dogs."

"Oh, I think we'll have peanut butter and jelly sandwiches then," said Mom, as she winked at me.

When Bruce left the room, I said, "He's a real corker, isn't he, Mom?"

"Yes, Joey. He's the kind of friend that requires much patience. Try to enjoy his uniqueness."

I just smiled at her remark. She writes poetry and

sometimes says flowery things. I generally ignore it. But it comes in handy when she checks my writing assignments. Most of the time she's easygoing, kind of soft. I think that's what makes her a good writer (and a good mom).

My newest model kept Bruce and me busy all afternoon. It was fun, but he had lots of stupid questions. It made me appreciate having a special, secret friend like the ghost. It was scary and thrilling to have Warren Hull all to myself. I changed the subject whenever Brucie mentioned the house. I said he'd learn all he wanted to when Dad talked to the class.

As we drove to the house on Saturday, my father started his usual riddle routine. He liked to challenge me with brain teasers.

"Yo, Joey, what is the very first thing ghosts do when they get in their cars?"

My head spun around when I heard the G word.

"I have no idea, Dad."

"Okay, they boo-cle up."

I chuckled. "Very good. Here's mine. What do you get when you cross a galaxy with a toad?"

"Hm, I give up."

"When you cross a galaxy and a toad you get Star Warts."

Dad laughed. "That's really a good one, Joe."

He pulled up in the driveway and said, "Remember, our visit to the house will be short today because of my meeting this afternoon."

"Right Dad, just call me whenever you're ready to leave."

I was eager to bring the ghost up to date and rubbed the glass quickly, with hard, willful strokes.

The cloudy pane cleared into the ghost's face.

"Joseph, how good to see you. You seem excited. Did you think of a way to help save my house?"

"Not really, but my dad is coming to school to talk about it to my class.

"By golden, that is a good beginning. I am sure you will think of something you can do."

"I hope so."

"Your willingness to try is half the battle. Remember the Proverb 'Trust in the Lord with all your heart.' Now, did you have other questions?"

"Yeah, I was wondering. Did your children go to school?"

"We taught them at home until the first log school was built in 1810 on Cemetery Road just north of Cayuga Creek Plank Road. Miss Freelove Johnson was the first teacher. She taught all grades together in one room. The building was also used for religious meetings. Sometimes evangelists came to preach and pray with the people and to celebrate the communion."

I whistled. "Boy, I can't believe how different things were then!"

"What more did you want to know, Joseph?"

"Did you see many Indians around here?"

"Yea, verily, there were many encounters, good and bad. My friend Ahaz had a frightening experience in 1804. He was away from home tending his grist mill on Cayuga Creek, working into the evening. His wife and six-year-old daughter were asleep in their cabin when a group of partying Indians entered the kitchen. They built a large fire and started a powwow."

"What's a powwow?"

"It's a ceremony with dancing and feasting. The mother managed to sneak her daughter out the window and sent her to get Ahaz. When he returned, there was a scuffle and he was able to chase them off.

The tribe was very impressed by his bravery. After that, they held him in great esteem and chiefs often consulted him concerning their problems."

"Man, that must have been scary!"

"Surely, but the natives were sometimes very helpful to the settlers. One winter, when our whole family was sick with influenza, a group of Indians— braves and their squaws—came to our cabin and showed us a curative procedure called 'Indian sweat.' They first dug holes in the ground, placed in stones that had been heated in a fire and then poured water over the rocks. They directed the family to sit around in a circle so we could breathe in the steam. They gave us warm drinks and bundled us up in blankets. The Indians tended to us all, replacing sweaty blankets until our fevers broke and we were able to care for ourselves. We may not have survived without their help. Thus many friendships blossomed, my lad."

I stood spellbound listening to the story. "Did you have trouble understanding the Indian language?"

"Ay-yup, but we had the help of Appolos Hitchcock, who was Indian Agent of the Cayuga Creek area. Both he and his son spoke the Seneca language fluently. They could interpret for us when the Indians wanted to barter for goods."

"What did you barter for?"

"We needed their fur for the cold winter and they wanted tools and beads. They were a proud and intelligent race. I particularly admired their version of

Psalm 23. Do you know it, Joseph? Its first sentence is The Lord is my shepherd."

"Yeah, we studied it in Religion class."

"Good. Let me see if I recall it now. Hum, hum."

"The Great Father above is the Shepherd Chief. I am his, and with him I want not. He throws out to me a rope, and the name of the rope is love, and he draws me and he draws me and he draws me to a place where the grass is green, and the water is good. I eat and lie down satisfied.

"Sometime, it may be very soon, it may be longer, it may be a long, long time, the Shepherd Chief will draw me to a place between mountains. It is dark there, but I will draw back not, I will be afraid not, for it is there between these mountains that the Shepherd Chief will meet me.

"Sometimes he makes the love rope into a whip, but afterward he gives me a staff to lean upon. He spreads before me a table with all kinds of food. He puts his hands upon my head, and all the tired is gone. My cup he fills until it runs over.

"What I tell you is true. I lie not. For these paths lead to the big teepee where dwells the Shepherd Chief, and after I die, I will live with him forever."

I shook my head and said, "Wow, that's neat!"

"Ay-up, it was favored by Native Americans because it helped them understand what Christian missionaries taught. Sometimes they called the higher power the Great Wisdom."

"It sure took a lot of courage to come here to live!"

"By golden it did, Joseph. One of the pioneers who preceded me came by himself at age twenty two with only fifty cents in his pocket. His sparse wardrobe was rolled into a bundle, tethered with a pin and dangled from the ax carried over his shoulder. He persevered and later owned 600 acres of land."

"I guess that proves all the hardships were worth it."

"Ay-up, that's why we all came, to have a chance for our own property. We were attracted by the fertile, level land of this region. The wood from the forests provided good timber for our homes."

"No wonder you want to preserve this house!"

"Yes, Joseph. It is a symbol of the struggle of many pioneers. There are many more stories to tell you, but someone is calling. I must leave you now."

He vanished as quickly as he had come.

Dad's voice intruded, "Joey, oh Joey. Time to leave."

"Coming Dad." I pushed my feet away, but I really wanted to stay and hear more stories.

Dad's visit to school was scheduled for next week, and I could hardly wait!

CHAPTER 4

On the day of Dad's visit to school, I was as nervous as before a swim meet.

Mr. Weston began, "Class, I'd like to introduce Mr. Peter Evans, Director of the Landmark Society of the Niagara Frontier. He's going to share some of his vast knowledge of Hull House, an important part of the history of our community."

Dad smiled. "Thank you, Mr. Weston. I see many familiar faces and I'm delighted to meet the rest of the class. Feel free to ask questions as I go along."

He picked up a piece of chalk. "Let's set the scene for Hull House. You know this area was originally the home of Eastern Woodland Indians. Did you know, however, that the Indians had a good sense of humor? The word Yankee actually came from an Indian word—Yanakie," he said, printing it on the board.

"It meant 'the silent one.' The Indians were so amazed at how much the pioneers talked that they called them 'yanakies' as a joke!"

The class laughed.

Richie mocked, "Big deal!"

Dad said, "Now, I have a riddle for you."

Oh no, Dad, I thought. Get to the house, please!

"The Woodland Indians sometimes used picture

writing to communicate. For instance, a hunter could leave a message on a tree at his camp to show which way he had gone, what he was going to do, like hunt beaver, for example, and how long he would be gone."

Dad moved to the blackboard. He wrote, – –. "Two marks = two days. Think about it. What was the major problem with this communication?" He looked around.

Richie bounced right out of his chair and yelled, "I got it! They didn't know when he left. So how would they know when two days were up?"

"Very good, Richie. Remember there were no calendars or clocks then. So they had to guess when the hunter departed."

Richie patted himself on the back and said, "I'm so smart!"

Murmurs echoed around the room. From then on, Richie seemed to pay more attention to Dad's talk.

Kristen raised her hand. "Were there Indians around when Hull House was built?"

"Yes, the Seneca Indians were here and many of them became friends of the pioneers."

I wanted to stand up and shout, yes! The ghost told me about them. But I swallowed so my secret wouldn't pop out.

Dad continued, "Now back to the year 1804 when the land at Genesee Street and Pavement Road was purchased by Warren Hull. He bought the land for $2 an acre from the Holland Land Company. Does anyone know the average price per acre now? Well, it's about $10,000 per acre for farmland and $30,000 for home property. Quite a difference, wouldn't you say?"

"Yeah, megabucks," said Richie.

Molly asked, "Did Warren Hull have a big family?"

"Oh yes, it was common then to have many children. They were needed to help with all the difficult chores of the pioneers. When he and his wife, Polly Gillet Hull arrived, they had seven daughters and three sons, and two more daughters were born here."

"Let's picture what the area looked like back then. The pioneers followed the Indians' well-worn paths and they are now generally our main east-west and north-south routes. Main Street was known as the Great Iroquois Trail."

Dad looked around at the kids and asked, "Does anyone here live on or near Broadway?"

Several hands went up.

Dad smiled. "Broadway was once known as the Cayuga Creek Plank Road and was a toll road. Toll booths, equipped with gates, were set up several miles apart. The gates blocked the road until travelers, in their horse-drawn wagons, paid the toll."

"How much was the toll?" asked Emily.

"The rate was 3¢ for a horse, 10¢ for horse and rider, 15¢ for horse and wagon, 25¢ for team and wagon, 7¢ for a dozen cattle and no charge for pedestrians."

The teacher said, "I'm sure the class realizes the difference in tolls now on the thruway."

Dad said, "Yes, things were different then in our town. The whole country was expanding rapidly too. In 1803, the government purchased 500,000,000 acres of land at 3¢ an acre. Who knows what state it became?"

Mike asked, "Was it Louisiana?"

"Sure was. Can anyone name the President at that time? No? There was a rhyme I learned as a boy:

'Thomas Jefferson, number three,
Rigged the sale of the century.'

What a bargain he got! Also in 1803, Ohio was admitted as the seventeenth state. In 1804, Lewis and Clark left St. Louis on an expedition to the Pacific. So this was the America that Warren Hull knew when he settled on Genesee Street. His first task was to clear the land and build a log cabin for his family. It wasn't until 1810 that the house you see there now was completed."

Claire said, "It looks like the covering on the house is falling off in spots. Is it stone?"

"Yes, Claire, it's limestone. There were many quarries around the area that were developed to supply limestone for the construction of mills, homes and bridges. I discovered a lime kiln close to Hull's lot. It included Lancaster Speedway and the other side of Gunville Road. It was eventually covered with fill and had gone into disuse by 1850. I found no record of it on old maps."

"Are you trying to repair the house?" asked Kristen.

"Yes, the Landmark Society's aim is to restore the house and ultimately use it for a museum."

Emily asked, "Are you working mostly on the outside?"

"So far, but there's much more to be done. I've been working to rebuild the chimney tops. I obtained small bricks from a condemned building in Buffalo. We want to be as close to the original in any renovation performed. I'm searching for some old glass to repair the windows. There probably are old window sashes rotting away somewhere."

Mr. Weston said, "It must cost quite a lot to make repairs. Has this been a problem?"

"Yes, it is a major factor. The Landmark Society has applied to the State for a $50,000 Environmental Bond for Historic Preservation Projects, but we have not yet received an answer."

"Please let us know when you do," replied the teacher.

Ted said, "Mr. Evans, I'm more interested in the inside of the house. How many rooms are there?"

"There are ten rooms and seven fireplaces. I have some drawings of the house layout. Would you like to see them?"

Kids nodded their heads and yelled yeah! Mr. Weston helped Dad attach the large sheets over the blackboard.

Dad said, "All right, let's have a look at the rooms."

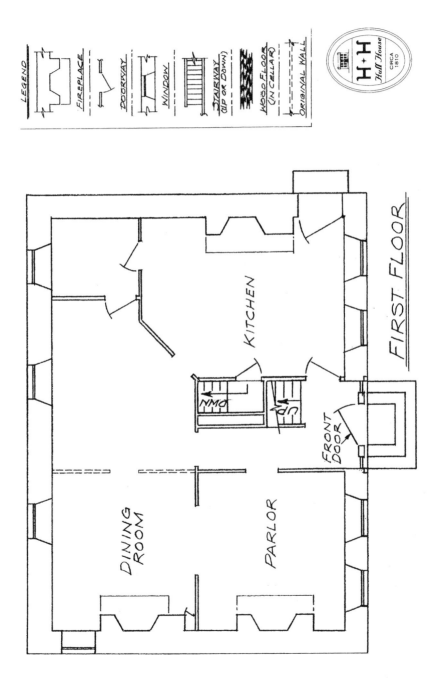

LEGEND

FIREPLACE
DOORWAY
WINDOW
STAIRWAY (UP OR DOWN)
WOOD FLOOR (IN CELLAR)
ORIGINAL WALL

H • H Hull House CIRCA 1810

FIRST FLOOR

KITCHEN

DOWN

UP

FRONT DOOR

DINING ROOM

PARLOR

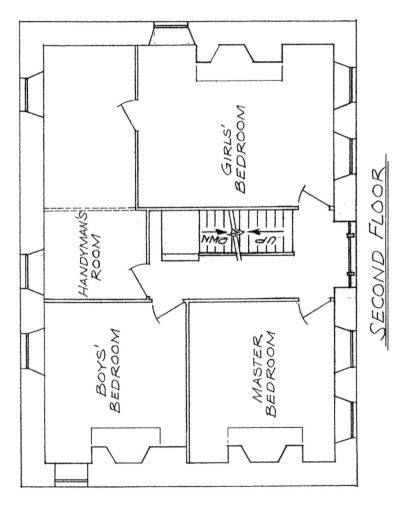

GIRLS' BEDROOM

HANDYMAN'S ROOM

DOWN UP

BOYS' BEDROOM

MASTER BEDROOM

SECOND FLOOR

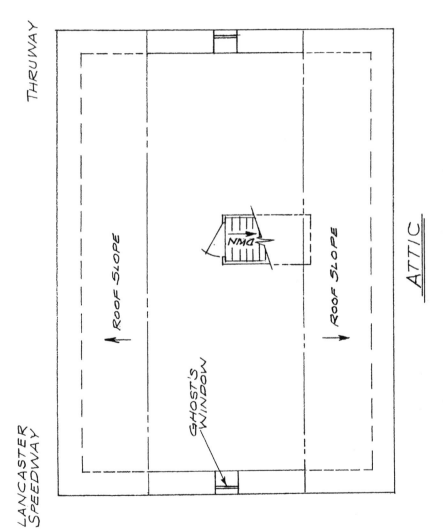

ATTIC

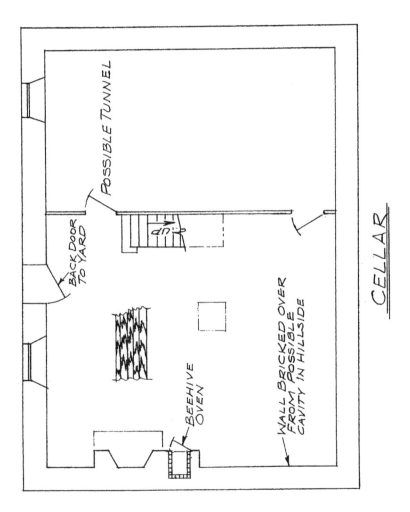

POSSIBLE TUNNEL

BACK DOOR TO YARD

UP

BEEHIVE OVEN

WALL BRICKED OVER FROM POSSIBLE CAVITY IN HILLSIDE

CELLAR

There were four drawings showing the first floor, second floor, attic and cellar. My eyes were focused on the ghost's window when Dad showed the attic. The kids asked lots of questions. I was sure they'd be even more fascinated if they knew Warren Hull was up there.

Bruce asked, "That little building in the back yard is an outhouse, isn't it?"

"Yes, there was no indoor plumbing, so the toilet was outside. It was sometimes called a privy. The early pioneers had to be resourceful and used dried corn cob as toilet paper."

The girls scrunched up their noses and said, "Eeeooo."

The boys laughed.

Dad continued. "Hull House was very sturdily built. It became important during the War of 1812 when the British burned Buffalo. People were fleeing in panic, carrying only meager belongings. Many headed out Genesee Street and the house provided a place of refuge for them."

Monica raised her hand. "My grandfather told me that this house was a station on the Underground Railroad and that maybe some of my ancestors were helped there. Like, maybe my great, great, great grandparents."

"Right, Monica. Around 1830, many local people were involved in transporting runaway slaves at night from one house to another, eventually crossing the

Niagara River into Canada. In the cellar of Hull House, just under the side door, we believe there was a tunnel. To the left of the fireplace, in the corner, the wall is bricked over and this could have led to a cavity in the hillside for hiding."

Monica's big brown eyes widened. "Gee, I'd really like to see that cellar."

Molly said, "Me too," and was echoed by several others.

"Dad, could our class visit the house?" I asked.

"It's fine with me. What about it, Mr. Weston?"

The teacher looked around the room. "How many would like to see the house?"

Every hand went up.

Mr. Weston raised his hands in amazement. "I guess it's unanimous! Can you arrange it soon? I think we have a great deal of enthusiasm here."

"Sure thing!" Dad began packing up, with applause and cheers from all the kids.

I was proud of him and put a big medal on his chest with my editing eye.

I made a wish that something good would come out of the class visit to Hull House. Maybe we COULD do something to save it!

CHAPTER 5

I picked up the mail at our box and ran in, waving an official-looking envelope with the State seal.

"Dad, Dad, this must be the answer you've been waiting for, about the house!"

"Here, let me see." As he opened the envelope, my eyes were glued to his hands. Dad was moving in slow motion and I wished I could fast-forward the process.

"Oh, no!" he said.

"What, Dad, what?"

"The news is not good, Joey. Our request has been denied. We will receive nothing for Hull House restoration."

"Nothing?"

"Right...zero...zilch." He threw the envelope down on the table.

My body was heavy as lead, like when I lost the swim meet at the YMCA. Dad placed an arm around my shoulder.

"I know this is not what we wanted to hear Joey, but we must not give up. We'll reapply to other sources. It's not the end of our dream; it just delays the process."

"But...where will you apply to?"

"Well, there are local foundations. It means I have

to do some research. Unfortunately, we do not have a famous name connection, like the architect Frank Lloyd Wright. This house represents the common man and his everyday life in history. How sad that the New York State Legislature declined to help with restoration of this unique property.

"I sure hope you find money somewhere."

"I'm going to try, son."

He reached in our cupboard for a couple of chocolate peanut butter cups. "Here, have one, it'll perk you up. Then we can get the chimney brick over to Hull House."

"Okay Dad." I munched on the candy and smiled. Ever since I was real little, Dad called it our "comfort food."

"By the way, Joey, I've arranged with your teacher to have the class visit Hull House next week."

"Great, Dad. The kids are really excited about seeing it. They sure are charged up since you gave your talk."

"Good. They realize we have a marvelous historic treasure right in our own back yard. A tremendous treasure!"

The drive over began in the usual way. "Yo, Joey. What would you call a history of cars?"

I wasn't in a riddle mood and shrugged my shoulders. "I don't know."

"An autobiography. Pretty good, eh?"

"Uh huh."

I helped him unload bricks from the trunk and

unlocked the front door. In the attic, I rubbed the glass and it felt warm from the sun. It was strange that even though the ghost was a spirit, he seemed like a real friend.

"Welcome, my lad, how goes it today?"

"Oh—well—I guess I have news for you, both good and bad news."

"Well, let's have the bad news first."

"My Dad had applied for aid from the state to pay for repairs to the house. Today he got an answer. They are not going to grant the Landmark Society any money at all."

"Pshaw, that's too bad. You seem very disappointed, young man."

"I am, but Dad says not to give up. He's going to try other sources, other foundations."

"You must heed your father's words. He is a very capable man. Now, what is your good news?"

"The good news is that my whole class is coming here to visit the house. All the kids want to come. I hope you like this idea."

"It is a good sign. We want more people to come and appreciate the house. I recall the words of a proverb, 'Hospitality is one form of worship.' So you must make them all feel welcome."

"Will it be all right for them to come up here to the attic?"

"Surely, but I will not communicate with you while they are present."

"That's what I figured."

"You and I can enjoy our visit today. Did you have more questions for me?"

"I was thinking about your twelve kids. What were their names?"

"Ah, the children. How odd to call them that. Kids were goats in my day."

He hummed. "The first two were girls—Polly and Rebecca. James was our first son. He answered the call to arms during the War of 1812."

"Dad said people escaping from the burning of Buffalo by the British stayed in this house."

"Ay-yup, James led them here, with only their clothes on their backs. We provided a place of refuge on a frigid December night."

"Your son must've been very brave."

"He was dependable and kind. When he married and moved to Kentucky, he put down roots and stayed. I was sore to see him go."

"You mean you were sad and missed him?"

"By golden I was. Anna was our fourth child. She married William Godfrey and their union ended sadly. Her husband was a soldier at Fort Niagara who shot a prisoner trying to escape. William was tried for murder and hanged in Lafayette Square in 1819. The sheriff did not want to execute him, but the law forced him to."

"Gross, he was just doing his job!"

"Ay-yup, justice was different in those days. Maria was

next, then sixth was Edmund, who remained a bachelor. He was a representative in the State Legislature, a very studious fellow. Hummm, I wonder how he would fathom this State funding business."

He continued humming. I asked, "Who was the seventh?"

"A boy—Justus. He had his own business making and selling bricks. He moved to Wisconsin in 1832."

"My dad is working on the chimney bricks right now."

"Bless your father's heart, lad."

"You had five more kids, right?"

"Ay-yup, all girls. Sophia, Miranda and Minerva were next. The last two—Aurilla and Vilera—were born here on this land."

When I heard Vilera's name, my mind raced back to the graveyard behind the house. I remembered seeing that only one headstone was left standing straight up. It was Vilera's!

I didn't think I should talk about the cemetery to him, so I gulped and said, "You sure have a bunch of dates and names to remember!"

"They are all engraved upon my memory like carvings on a tree, and they are all entwined in this house. That is why it must be saved. Hark! Do you hear something?"

Dad's voice boomed up to the attic, "Joey, I'm quitting!"

"Coming Dad. Mr. Hull, I have to leave now. When I come back, it will be with the whole class."

"Good, I will be watching." He became fuzzy as he said his last "Farewell."

⊷ ⊷ ⊷

Back home, I grabbed a can of root beer and popped open the lid. I guzzled the cool bubbly liquid. It helped wash Hull House dust from my throat. My worries didn't end there, though. Mom called me to come up to my room and I didn't like the ice in her voice.

She was waiting for me, hands on hips, eyebrows scrunched together. I knew that look meant Big Trouble.

"Joseph, I came to your room to gather dirty laundry. I could hardly find it in this mess. What a disaster area!"

"But Mom, I've been busy."

"No excuses, young man. You get started immediately on the clean up. Don't come out until you can see the floor and furniture tops. And never mind 'stuffing' things in your closet. Remember last month when everything fell out when I opened the closet door?"

"Yes Mom, I remember."

"Good. Also remember it caused you to be grounded for a week."

"Yes, Mom." I knew better than to argue at this point.

Her top was really blowing, like a volcano. I revised the scene, removed the smoke and calmed her down.

I whistled for Libby to come upstairs. At least she'd keep me company. I could always count on her loyalty. She was the only one who didn't mind my stinky sneakers. Andrea, especially, was always pinching her nose and saying "Eeeooo" whenever she was near them.

My thoughts were still on Hull House as I got the cleanup job done. Inspector Mom okayed my work and I was finally off the hook. Man, why do these weird things keep happening to me?

CHAPTER 6

As usual, Richie was Mr. Big Shot on the bus ride to Hull House.

He boasted, "I bet I'll see the ghost first! My eyes are sharp and I'll be on the ball. Just in case someone else spots him, call me and I'll take over."

Brucie said, "Mr. Weston told us the ghost is just a rumor."

Richie started his mocking laugh. "Just be careful in the attic, Brucie. He might snatch you there!"

Other kids answered, "Shut up Richie, knock it off."

I wished I could tell them that the ghost wasn't scary. My worry was that Richie might ruin the day with his loud mouth. I knew I had to keep an eye on him, especially in the attic.

Dad stood in the doorway as the class filed off the bus and up the walkway. "Welcome, welcome, come right in!"

Mr. Weston followed the class and they sat on the floor. "Ready, Mr. Evans?"

"Sure. Kids, if you recall the drawing we looked at, this is the living room. Called the 'parlor' in those days, it was usually reserved for drinking tea and entertaining friends."

"Next is the dining room. The hearth has been

removed from the fireplace, but you can see the tea kettle crane, even though it's jammed at present. There's a small cupboard built in on the left."

Emily said, "They probably kept tea cups and saucers there."

"Right. Get up and move along, class. Notice the original floors are six inches wide, tongue and groove."

Claire asked, "What does that mean, Mr. Evans?"

"It means a protruding strip along the edge of a board that fits into a matching groove on the edge of another board. So they are joined without using nails."

"Neat," said Claire, "like a puzzle."

Dad said, "Initially the front entrance led through to the back outside door. Next is the utility room and then the kitchen, which faces the front. Originally, a large stone fireplace extended three feet into the kitchen."

"Sounds like it was changed a lot," said Mr. Weston.

"Yes, an addition was put on in 1860 and the window was made into a door on the left of the fireplace. Plumbing and electricity were added much later."

Dad led the way to the staircase. "As we go upstairs, notice the cherry handrail. The ledge at the top of the stairs was probably for a grandfather clock."

Dad waited for the class to file into the front room. "Here the floors and window frames are original. This first bedroom over the parlor is the master bedroom.

Back of it is a smaller bedroom with a little fireplace where the three boys slept."

Walking out, he said, "Next to it is a very small room with wide pine floor boards and no fireplace. It was probably used by the hired hand and must have been freezing cold in the winter time. Imagine washing your face and hands in a water basin with ice in it! There were no water faucets to turn on, kids, let alone hot water."

Bruce said, "Ooh, I would turn into an icicle myself!"

The class laughed. Someone said, "Leave it to Brucie!"

"These rooms on the other side, above the kitchen, were originally one large bedroom that went from front to back. We believe all the girls slept here together. You will recall there were nine girls in all."

"My goodness, how did they possibly fit all nine in one bedroom?" asked Kristen.

Dad smiled. "They probably slept three in a bed. At least they stayed warmer during the winter."

"Let's climb the stairs to the attic. They are rather steep, so take your time and be careful. Notice that the entrance has a very plain plank door with a steel bar latch. Come in and check out the forty foot long hand hewn beams overhead. If you look up, you can see the ax strokes made by Warren Hull and his three sons."

Richie said, "It must've been fun to chop the wood for those rafters. I wish I lived in those days."

I kept watching Richie. So far he seemed to have forgotten ghost bugging.

Dad answered, "It was a lot of hard work, Richie. Look down and see the fifteen inch wide floor boards here. They are quite a bit wider than the other parts of the house."

I wondered what the ghost was thinking. I held my breath as Brucie went over to his window and peered out.

He said, "Wow, you can see Lancaster Speedway from here, just like you said, Joey."

Dad waved his arm, "Time to go back down and I'll lead you to the cellar. The stairs in the kitchen are wobbly, so we'll go outside."

The class followed Dad downstairs and out the door. We entered the downstairs kitchen from ground level.

Richie said, "This house is neat, with all these doors and stairs."

When everyone was in the cellar, Dad said, "Notice the split wooden ceiling and stone paneled walls. The bake oven to the left of the fireplace is brick lined. Its circular shape is curved into the wall. It is known as a beehive oven and is one of the oldest surviving cooking fireplaces. All the cooking in the summer was done down here, to keep the rest of the house cool."

Bruce said, "Good idea. I don't like being too hot!"

Dad continued, "You can see the uneven floor boards here. The widest board is twenty-six inches.

Can you imagine how big the tree they used for this must have been?"

"Yeah, humongous!" said Richie.

"Underneath this floor is a cistern seven feet deep," said Dad.

"What's a cistern, Mr. Evans?" asked Mike.

"It's a tank for catching and storing rainwater. That water was used for bathing and cleaning. Water for cooking and drinking came from the well outside."

Monica said, "Mr. Evans, where is the hiding place for the Underground Railroad?"

"Right here, Monica, next to the door. It has been bricked over. Another possibility is to the left of the fireplace in the corner. It could have led to a cavity in the hill. We can only guess now, because no written documentation has been found."

"Did Warren Hull leave a diary or letters?" asked Kristen.

"No, unfortunately. Wouldn't it be wonderful if he had?"

I made a mental note to ask the ghost about a diary and the Underground Railroad.

Dad turned and walked over to the stairs. "Let's go back up and I'll answer any other questions you may have."

We filed back to the living room and sat on the floor. Immediately, many hands went up.

Mike said, "Mr. Weston told us that the State isn't giving any money for house repairs. Could it be torn down?"

"Well, it was listed on the National Register of Historic Places in 1992. The following year, the Landmark Society was granted title to the property on the condition that restoration work would begin within ten years. So it is important that funds be found soon."

Mr. Weston looked at all the concerned faces and said, "Let's brainstorm and see if we can come up with suggestions to solve the problem. We've had success doing that in class in the past."

Richie raised his hand. "We could try to find some rich guy who would donate lots of money."

Molly asked, "Mr. Weston, couldn't we have a fund-raiser?"

"That's a great idea! Every little bit helps. How would we go about it, class?"

Claire said, "My parents sell houses and they always say the best way to show off a building is to have open house."

"Yeah, we could have our own open house right here and invite people to come," said Mike.

Emily said, "Maybe we could sell refreshments and earn some money to pay for repairs."

"We could have a bake sale!" said Molly.

Mike said, "We could sell lemonade."

"How about pioneer punch?" laughed Richie.

"That's not a bad idea," answered the teacher. "We could do some research and find a recipe."

"Maybe we could dress in costumes," Kristen offered.

"Another good reason for research," nodded the teacher.

The kids buzzed like bees with each new idea.

"How about music?" asked Claire. "It's always nice to have background music."

"That's a good suggestion. Bruce's Mom is a music teacher and perhaps she could find some appropriate tapes. What do you think, Bruce? Brucie?"

Mr. Weston's eyes scanned the roomful of kids. "Where is he? Has anyone seen Bruce lately?"

They all looked around, puzzled, but no one remembered seeing Bruce.

The teacher grew pale. "He must be here somewhere. Let's search each room. I want no one wandering around by himself, so choose a partner."

Mike and I teamed up.

Dad said, "I'll check outside. He may have strayed when we came back from the basement."

Dad went out the front door and circled outside to the back yard. He called, "Bruce, Bruce." He heard a voice and followed the sound. It led him to the outhouse.

"Help, help me! It's me, Brucie. Help, help."

Dad tapped on the back window where he saw my teacher and yelled, "He's out here."

At the outhouse, Dad yelled, "Brucie, are you in there?"

"Yeah, I am. I'm stuck! The latch on the door won't open and I'm locked in!"

The teacher bounded out the door followed by bunches of kids. "Where is he, Pete?"

"In the outhouse, Ward. He apparently has a problem with the latch."

"Brucie, are you all right?" Mr. Weston hollered.

"Yeah, I'm okay. Just get me out of this stinky old place."

Kids were laughing. The teacher gave them a stern look and some covered their mouths to keep from laughing out loud.

Dad pressed on the outside of the old door. "Brucie, just take your hand off the latch and see if this pressure loosens it a bit, okay?"

"All right."

"Now, as I push, see if you can pull up on the handle."

"Oh, it clicked. Let's see—yeah—it seems looser now. Yeah, it's opening."

Brucie came out to a chorus of cheers and hoots from the class. His chubby face was beet red and he was still pinching his nose shut. "I could ardly breed in dere. I dought I'd die from the fumpes."

Richie and a few other boys were laughing so hard, they were rolling on the grass. The two adults had grins on their faces. Girls were giggling so hard, they began to dance around.

Mr. Weston cleared his throat. "What were you doing there anyway?"

"Well, the bathroom was busy and I had to go, so I thought I'd try the outhouse."

The teacher said, "Let's all get back inside. Remember, no one is to ever wander off alone again!"

Gradually, the class quieted down, but not without a few more snickers. Seated on the living room floor, they looked to Mr. Weston for direction.

The teacher said, "We were planning an open house here, Bruce, to sell things. We'd like to have music. Could you ask your mother if she has any tapes of music popular in the early 1800's?"

"Sure. Her collection is really big."

"Good, let us know soon. Mr. Evans, it looks as if my class wants to adopt Hull House as their cause. Do you think it might help?"

"I'm certain it will. It's about time we got young people involved in preserving a piece of our local history. Your idea of an open house is super. Let's come up with a date—a Sunday, perhaps?"

My face almost hurt from smiling during the whole visit. It was like watching a play unfold before my eyes, and the ending was just perfect.

CHAPTER 7

After Saturday chores and swim practice, Dad and I headed for Hull House.

"Yo, Joey, what was the colonists' favorite tea?"

"Got me, Dad,"

"Liberty, son, liber*ty*."

I laughed. "That reminds me of one. Did Thomas Jefferson make his own coffee?"

"I don't know."

"No, it was too much of a grind."

Dad chuckled. "I called your teacher this morning and we scheduled the Open House for Sunday, May 26th."

"Great! Now we have to get people to come."

"Advertising should help you do that, Joey."

"Maybe a newspaper ad would help."

"Can't hurt, Joe. Think about it."

I helped him unload tools from the car. "I guess I'll go inside and goof around."

"OK, remember I'm not working too long today."

I hurried upstairs to talk to the ghost.

Applying pressure to the glass was like dialing a friend's telephone number. He answered his call more quickly this time. Practice makes perfect, I guess.

"Hello, Joseph. How are you today?"

"Great. My class is really excited after the tour with Dad. They want to help save the house."

"That is good news! I was bamboozled to see so many young ones exploring here."

"Yeah, they had fun. There is something I wondered about, though. Dad said this house was used as a station on the Underground Railroad. Do you know about this?"

"Ay-yup. My youngest daughter, Vilera, helped to feed, clothe and shelter fugitives. We were all sympathetic to the cause and were glad to help slaves escape to Canada."

"Did you keep a diary or any record of this?"

"No, Joseph. Few people kept any clues that might be incriminating. Everything had to be kept secret."

"Do you think your daughter had a diary?"

"Hmm, not a diary, but I do recall something. She was very secretive by nature and tended to hide things. Perhaps if you search around in the girls' bedroom, you may find something. There was a loose brick in the fireplace where she kept treasures. I do not know what survives today."

"Great! I'll have to look there!"

"What else was on your mind, lad?"

"Dad said winters were icy cold in the bedrooms."

"Oh indeed. Even many blankets did not help in the midst of bitter cold. Polly would use a warming pan with a few hot embers from the fire to pass between the sheets. It had to be kept moving or it would scorch them."

"Did your kids hate winter?"

"Ay-yup, in some ways. They knew that misbehavior might result in being sent to this frigid attic to shell beans. Once I found Edmund and Justus having a snowball fight up here. The southwest corner let in more than a draft."

"They must have been freezing!"

"They did have some fun, though, when they skated on frozen ponds. We made blades of wood or iron and strapped them to their boots."

"My sister and I go skating all year on an inside rink."

"Hmm, I do not comprehend, my lad."

"A rink is a skating pond inside a building," I explained.

"Do tell, what an odd notion!"

"Mr. Hull, our class is adopting your house as a project. We'll have an open house in a few weeks and sell stuff to raise money."

"By golden, what an excellent idea. A frolic in this old house will be welcome. What things will you sell?"

"Mostly food and drinks. My teacher says we have to make old fashioned....I mean....stuff you ate. It would be great to earn some money for repairs."

"Even if your earnings are meager, you will be helping other people learn our history. A proverb comes to mind. 'Commit your work to the Lord, and your plans will be established.'"

"Oh, I almost forgot. We may play some music at the open house. Is that okay?"

"Of course. We all liked music. My cousin held our first singing school in a hollow buttonwood tree. The hollow was big enough for a man to stand upright in. They made benches inside and cut holes to admit the light. When young folks sang, it sounded as if they were in an arched room."

"Wow, that must have been some huge tree!"

"It was almighty for the carryings-on, especially singing my favorites 'Barbara Allen' and 'Old Dan Tucker.'"

"My dad'll be coming soon. I'm not sure when I'll be back because he has some Saturday meetings scheduled."

"Then vamoose. Reckon you have much work to do, praise the Lord!"

As his image faded, I turned and ran down the stairs. I felt light enough to float down, just like a ghost.

———— ⚔✦⚔ ————

At school on Monday, everyone was talking about the open house. Ideas flew around like fireflies on a July night.

Mr. Weston said, "We have a little more work on our Ethnic Festival before we can devote all our efforts to the open house."

"Shoot, we've spent enough time on that project already," said Richie.

"We'll wrap it up on Friday with our auditorium performance. Make sure your costumes are ready, class."

He moved to the blackboard. "Let's plan ahead with some important dates." He wrote:

Hull House

Open House May 26—Research due May 4

"This is the basic plan. Every idea must be backed up by proof from research. For instance, if you want to show how settlers' children played a game of marbles, you must find an example in your research. Remember to list your sources. This will be due in ten days. Any questions?"

"Does it have to be a long report?" asked Emily.

"No, use outline form. Would anyone like to share an idea now?"

Molly said, "My mom has a doll collection and she has two colonial types. One is named Dolley, after Dolley Madison. She's dressed very plainly with a soft cap. The other is Josephine. She's fancier with a poke bonnet. Could I show them at the open house?"

"Sure. Perhaps your research could be on clothes."

Claire said, "My mother has an embroidered sampler that was stitched by my great aunt. It has a poem on it. I wrote it down:

'Kindly words
Will cost but little
Traveling up the hill of life
And they make
The weak and weary
Stronger, braver for the strife'"

"Excellent, Claire. You could display that and do research on pioneer girls' sewing. You might include the popularity of proverbs also."

I wished they could hear the ghost's proverbs. It would've been great to let everything I knew gush out. The effort to keep the secret felt like holding back Niagara Falls inside me.

Molly said, "What kind of parties did they have then?"

The teacher answered, "They had work/play parties called bees. Some were for barn raising, corn husking or quilting."

Emily said, "My grandma belongs to the Historical Society. Maybe I could borrow a quilt to show."

Kristen waved her hand, dangling something from her wrist. It looked soft and old. "I brought this antique purse my grandma gave me. It's called a reticule. She said many ladies used these drawstring pouches in olden days. Maybe we could sew some purses like this and sell them at the Open House!"

All the girls oohed and ahhed saying, "Yeah!"

The teacher responded, "Awesome idea, Kristen!"

Richie shouted, "I'd like to know what sports kids played then."

"I'm sure you'd enjoy that. One popular game was quoits, where metal rings were tossed at an iron stake set in the ground. Poorer people used old horseshoes."

"Maybe I could set up a game of horseshoes behind the house and charge a quarter to play," said Richie.

"If we have good weather, it would work. They also played nine pin bowling, checkers, dominoes and cards. Another popular game was huzzlecap, where they pitched pennies in a jar."

Ted waved his hand. "I could run a game pitching pennies. People really liked it at our church bazaar!"

"That would probably be a crowd pleaser, Ted," replied Mr. Weston.

Joni said, "My mom offered to help me bake something."

I said, "We could make cookies in the shape of the house. My grandpa offered to make a cookie cutter for us."

The teacher smiled. "Super idea!"

"We could call them Hull House cookies and sell them at the open house," I said.

Brucie murmured, "Boy, I'd buy some of those!"

Mr. Weston asked, "Bruce, did you check the music?"

"Yeah, Mom has a tape of music popular in the 1800's."

"Good. Our project is starting to shape up."

Nicole raised her hand. "Would an invitation be a good idea? I could print it on our computer."

Wow, I should have thought of that! Nicole is our class computer expert. Her dad has a real neat setup, with a color printer and scanner. She was my partner for a project and it was fun working with her, even if she *is* a girl.

"Good thinking, Nicole," Mr. Weston said.

Nicole's face beamed like sun on water. "Maybe Joey and I could work together on the invitation."

Richie mocked, "Ooh, Joey."

Mr. Weston slapped the chalk down on the tray. "Enough about parties. Math books out! Turn to page 61."

Richie banged his book onto his desk and slammed it shut, grumbling, "I hate math! Hull House is more fun."

Many in the class groaned, unwilling to let go of the open house ideas, even for a day.

I knew how they felt. That's all I could think of too. If I had known what problems were coming, I would have been worried.

CHAPTER 8

I biked over to the Public Library after school. My bike wanted to race and I let it. My research had become a mission. The ghost had started it; now it was up to me to help save the house. It was fun to use my own brain to make things work. It made me feel like I was helping.

Nicole met me at 4 o'clock. We checked the catalog and shelves for books on the 1800's and both left with an armful. At home, I dumped the books on my desk and whistled for my dog. "Exercise time, Libby."

Libby played her trick with the Frisbee. She ran back to me, holding on to the disk, shaking her head back and forth, teasing me to take it from her. She growled contentedly before letting it go for another pass.

I praised her after each throw with "Good dog." When she was winded and panting, I bent down and put my arms around her neck.

"Things are getting better," I whispered. "The ghost knows we're trying to help, old pal."

Libby's response was a satisfied whimper. She slurped her wet tongue against my cheek. It felt warm and fuzzy, like soft, sticky sandpaper.

At school on Friday, the whole class wore costumes for our Ethnic Festival. Girls wore long skirts, shawls and aprons. The boys wore suspenders and caps to look like immigrants. We had done research on our ancestors and country of origin. We were going to present a play that afternoon in the auditorium.

We had gym class in the morning, but it worked out okay because we were square dancing.

Mr. Sully, our gym teacher, made his class fun. He always goofed around and told us about his awards for speed skating at Lake Placid.

As usual, Richie acted like such a jock and showed off in gym. He liked to brag about being captain of the Hornets basketball team and winning the 'Iron Kid' award on Sports Night. That really puffed him up! Mr. Sully was usually pretty patient with him, but on this day, he lost it.

We were do-si-do-ing in our sets, swinging around, when Monica's long skirt started sliding down her hips. Big mouth Richie pointed at her and yelled, "Oooh!"

Monica grabbed her skirt and ran over to Miss Broadly, the lady gym teacher. She had tears in her eyes and a big safety pin in her hand. It must have opened up while she danced. Luckily, she caught her skirt just in time.

Mr. Sully really tore into Richie and sent him to the office. I was glad he got what he deserved.

My imagination edited the scene, dunking Richie in a water tank for punishment.

After the Ethnic Festival performance, Mr. Weston said, "Now on to our open house plans. Everyone has completed project outlines. Several students will have actual examples of pioneer items to display. Others will do a drawing to illustrate their contribution. Try to learn all you can about your presentation so you may answer questions easily at the open house. Joey, did you make any headway with the cookie cutter?"

"Yeah, Grandpa is making the cutter out of tin. Mom and my sister will try it out this weekend."

"Excellent. Bruce, will your mother provide a tape player for the music?"

"Sure, but I'd like to know....about the cookies.... What flavor will they be?"

Richie mocked, "There goes Burger, thinking about food again!"

Giggles passed from one kid to another, like echoes in a cave.

I glanced over to the Open House Invitation on the chalk tray. Nicole and I had done a pretty neat job together, I thought. My sister had teased me about working a whole Sunday afternoon with a girl. "So what?" I said. "Some girls have brains, Andrea."

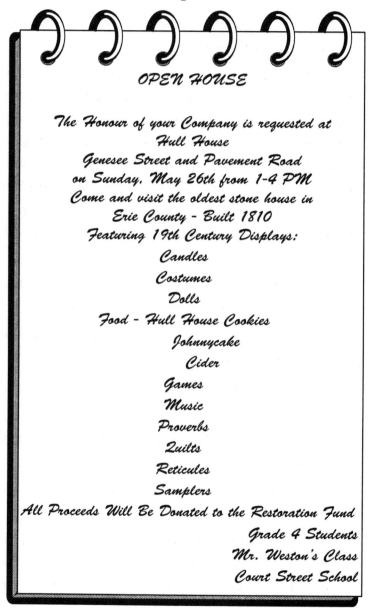

OPEN HOUSE

The Honour of your Company is requested at
Hull House
Genesee Street and Pavement Road
on Sunday, May 26th from 1-4 PM
Come and visit the oldest stone house in
Erie County - Built 1810
Featuring 19th Century Displays:
Candles
Costumes
Dolls
Food - Hull House Cookies
Johnnycake
Cider
Games
Music
Proverbs
Quilts
Reticules
Samplers
All Proceeds Will Be Donated to the Restoration Fund
Grade 4 Students
Mr. Weston's Class
Court Street School

Mr. Weston pointed to the chart. "Okay, let's examine our invitation. Nicole and Joey provided a fine outline including our list of projects. Kristen, have you made plans for the reticules?"

Kristen smiled. "Yes, I'm going to work with Claire. She's very good at sewing. We'll choose material at the fabric store and my mom will show us how to make the reticules."

The teacher made a thumbs-up sign. "It'll fit right in with the girls wearing bonnets, muffs, and hooded capes. Now, let's look at the invitation to fine-tune it."

Ted asked, "Who will get the invitations?"

"Each of you will receive one for your family. I would like to have enough for the other two fourth grades. Nicole, will you be able to print about one hundred?"

"No problem. Could we put it in the *Lancaster Bee?* My parents said lots of people in town read it."

"Good idea! I'll stop in there with an invitation. The next step is to practice our projects in front of the class. Let's prepare for that by using a proverb, 'The early bird catches the worm.' I think our early start will ensure a successful open house."

There go those proverbs again!

The ghost's words about his daughter and the Underground Railroad kept buzzing around my brain. I was glad when Dad said he was making a quick stop at Hull House.

There was no time to go to the attic, but I did race up to the girls' bedroom. I went straight to the fireplace. My hands felt along the left side but everything seemed solid.

I found myself wishing I could bring Libby here so she could smell around and find something. Dad told me Labs sniffed out booby traps and mines for the soldiers in World War II. But I had to do this myself.

I moved to the right side. About halfway down, a brick wobbled. I pushed and pressed, but it wouldn't budge. Keep trying, I thought, this must be it! Finally, the brick popped out. At the back of the hole was a small box. My hands shook as I lifted it. Dad called and I almost dropped it. I stuffed it in my jacket pocket and replaced the brick.

I turned and yelled, "Coming Dad."

I could hardly wait until I was alone in my room to open the box. It was made of wood and had something engraved on top. I rubbed the dust off and my fingers traced the letters VH. Of course—the initials for Vilera Hull!

I opened the cover and inside was a curious little pin. It had a picture of two hands, one white, one black, on a book. I have to show this to Dad, I thought. He doesn't have to know how I found it.

ANONYMOUS
ABOLITIONIST BUTTON
1840s - 50s
Daguerreotype
Diameter 1.6 cm (⅝ in.)

Gilman Paper Company Collection.

I called him to my room. I explained that I found the box while I was poking around in the house.

He said, "Joey, this is quite a find! It's an abolitionist's button. That's a Bible the two hands are on. I saw a photo of it in an exhibit at the Metropolitan Museum of Art. It's a symbol of opposition to slavery."

He turned it over and over in his hand. "This is a daguerreotype. It has to be over 150 years old."

"What's a daguerreotype?"

"It's an early photographic process. Notice that the picture is set in a metal frame. It has a loop on the reverse so it can be sewn onto clothing. A phone call to the Museum in New York City should give us more details."

I said, "Look at the initials on the box, Dad. It must have belonged to Vilera Hull, the youngest daughter."

"Why, Joe, how did you figure that out?"

"Uh, well, I remember you showed me a list of the family names and V H fits the last one."

I thought, wow, that was a close call. My secret about the ghost almost popped out. I pushed it back down just in time! *Edit—Erase those words!*

"This is exciting!" said Dad. "Did you know the word photography comes from the Greek? It means 'writing with light.' We have gotten a message from the past, Joey."

Dad was eager to tell the Landmark Society about it, and I was eager to tell the ghost. Was this a good sign?

CHAPTER 9

"Boy, Mom, do those cookies smell good!" My nose led me to the kitchen after swim practice on Saturday morning.

"Hi Joey, hope they taste as good! Andrea and I have finished the first batch. Maybe you'd like to help decorate them."

Andrea said, "The frosting is the fun part, Joey. We can work as a team. The red twist candy has to be cut for the chimneys. I'm mixing the frosting now."

"Hang on, Andrea, quit bossing. I'll get there."

"The cookie cutter works great, Joey," said Mom.

All afternoon, we mixed dough, rolled it out, cut the houses and decorated them. Each batch made three dozen cookies.

As Mom was cleaning up, she sighed. "It will take forever to finish enough cookies. I think we need to get other families involved, Joey. Perhaps another mom would like to use the cookie cutter during the week, while I'm at work. We only have about 100 cookies here and I'm sure we'll need more."

"Maybe Grandpa can make more cookie cutters," said Andrea.

"We could ask him," I said, "but the first one took lots of time. How much do you think we can get for them, Mom?"

"Well, the large cookies at the Mall are $1.19 apiece. I think we could charge $1.25 for the fund-raiser."

"It would be better if we got more. We really want to make a profit for the house." *My video eye saw dollar bills falling from the sky and covering Hull House.*

"I know, Joey, but we have to be reasonable," replied Mom.

The phone rang, and it was Mike asking me to play basketball. I was tempted but I told him I couldn't because something important was going on at home. I was glad he didn't push for an explanation. I didn't want him to think I was a nerd for working on the cookies.

The following week, Mom found two other families willing to bake cookies, so we ended up with 300. In school, the kids practiced their presentations. Invitations were handed out and a copy was published in the *Lancaster Bee.* The kids were as wired as if Christmas was coming.

Everyone hoped that the weather would improve and erase the cold and rainy system stalled in the area. We had outdoor plans too.

May 26 finally arrived.

When we got to the house, Mom (the poet) said, "All our wishes have been answered with the dawning of this beautiful May day. Spring's voice has matured from a whisper to a shout."

Dad smiled. "The house seems to be saying Welcome. Look at all those kids with parents and grandparents. Super!"

As we walked from our car, mom exclaimed, "Oh, what beautiful lilac bushes! I'm going to cut some to take inside."

She grabbed my sister's hand. "Come hold them as I cut, Andrea. I read that pioneer women liked to spread their laundry over these bushes to dry and capture the scent. Wasn't that a good idea?"

"The flowers must have made things smell pretty," said Andrea.

Inside, everyone was as busy as a beaver.

Richie ran in. "Mr. Weston, the lawn bowling and horseshoe games are set up. The two pairs of stilts my Dad made work great!"

"Fine, Richie," the teacher replied. "Make sure the stilts are used only when an adult is present."

He looked over to the tables filled with baked goods, tea and cider. "Bruce, will you stop salivating over there and help your family set up the music area?"

Brucie blushed. "Okay, I was just trying to figure out how many things I could buy. Those cookies sure look good!"

Mom said, "This whole house is wrapped in a medley of folk music, as if it was tied with a beautiful ribbon of sound."

She walked over to Bruce's mom. "Mrs. Burger, thank you for that finishing touch."

Mrs. Burger smiled. "You're welcome. I always think of Longfellow's words about music being the universal language of mankind."

"It really does communicate a sense of the nineteenth century," said Mom.

By one o'clock, guests began arriving. Each room had students stationed with their displays. Girls, dressed in long skirts, bonnets, aprons, and shawls, smiled while they worked. They used costumes left over from our Ethnic Festival. I was glad to see Monica wore a big belt to hold up her skirt.

Molly had the old dolls in the large bedroom, along with Claire's samplers and Emily's quilts. Kristen lined up the colorful reticules on a table and sold them quickly.

In the other bedroom, people lined up to play corn-cob checkers or pitch pennies. Even the youngest kids tried to get pennies to land in jars Ted set up in a row.

Mike and I were tour guides. We explained the uses of the rooms and described Warren and Polly Hull's family.

When Mr. Weston announced it was four o'clock, I could hardly believe it.

Dad said, "Ward, I think your open house was quite a success. Parents are tallying up the receipts now."

Mr. Weston nodded. "I'm sure community consciousness was raised today, Pete. I hope this is a harbinger of a positive future for this old house."

After most visitors had gone, Richie suggested the class have a stilt contest. "We could have two people on a team and see who can stay up the longest."

Mr. Weston approved the idea and said to choose numbers to get partners. "That should be more fair," he said.

When Bruce and I both drew number three, Richie mocked, "Wow, what a team, a Brainiac and a Burger, ha, ha!"

The teacher gave a stern look. "All right, that's enough, Richie. I'll time each pair with my stop watch and keep score."

All the kids had a great time balancing on the stilts, even if they couldn't stay up long. When Bruce and I got up, I shouted, "Doin' good, Bruce. Maybe we can beat Richie's and Ted's time."

Bruce worked hard to balance and surprised everyone.

Someone yelled, "Go, go, go!" Soon the whole class chanted.

Suddenly, Bruce wavered and wailed, "Whoa!" He tilted forward, then sideways, and fell back with a crash to the grass. He crawled onto his knees and howled, "Oh, no!" He puffed, grunted and grabbed at his back.

I jumped down and ran over to him. "Brucie, are you hurt?"

He just bawled louder and shook his head. "No, but, but!"

"It's okay, Bruce. You were terrific. You were up a long time, almost as long as Richie. You have nothing to be ashamed of."

Bruce buried his head in his hands and mumbled, "It's not that, Joe. I had cookies in my pockets and I just smashed them. I was saving them to eat later!"

I turned away and said, "Oh Bruce, you're weird!"

CHAPTER 10

Everything was going so smoothly, my whole body was buoyant. It was like floating on my back in a peaceful pool. That feeling sunk away when I heard my father talking on the phone the next day.

"This does not bode well for the future of the house, I'm afraid," he said grimly.

Now what? Just when things were lookin' good after our fund-raiser. I could hardly wait for him to get off the phone.

"What's wrong, Dad?"

"A large supermarket chain has chosen Lancaster as the site for a huge grocery distribution center. Company representatives are submitting a rezoning request to town officials."

"What does rezoning mean?"

"Each town designates areas for a particular type of building. Right now, the Supermart area is zoned as farmland. If a business is to be put there, the Town Board must approve it and change the zone to commercial."

"Why are you so worried?"

"They want to put it just across from Hull House and they plan to widen Genesee Street. I hope that the National Registry will protect the house, but this massive project is bound to affect the neighborhood."

He shook his head sadly. "Sometimes it seems as if the future of the house is as precarious as those homes in California being eaten up by brush fires. One more lick and it could be gone forever."

"This sounds serious."

"It is, Joey, but we may get help from some of the neighbors who are not happy about the project. At this point, it's still just a proposal before the Town Board."

"Maybe the Board won't approve."

"I don't know, son. We'll have to wait and see what happens."

My editing eye saw Hull House in a tug of war with Supermart's huge warehouse. The little guy won!

In the car, Dad said, "We have a good start with community awareness. We have to keep up the fight to save Hull House. Hey, speaking of a fight, Joey, did George Washington fight bear?"

"I don't know, Dad. Did George Washington fight bear?"

"No. He fought dressed."

"Groan! I should have gotten that one. Wow, look how empty the house looks today!"

"Yep, we sure had a good crowd yesterday."

Once inside, my feet barely touched the steps as I rushed to the attic. I rubbed the window pane and wondered what to tell the ghost first.

"Welcome, Joseph, I've been waiting for you. Your carryings-on sure attracted a boodle of people. This house fairly sang with joy to have all that life here."

"Yeah, it was a super turnout. Our class raised $600 for the restoration!"

"By golden, that is quite an accomplishment. Sounds like things are looking up."

"Well, there are some new problems. A supermarket wants to build a huge warehouse not far from here."

"What is a supermarket?"

"It's a big store that sells all kinds of food and other stuff. My dad is worried about the future of the house because they plan to widen the road."

"Dash it all! This could mean trouble!"

"Yeah, dad says it's a gigantic project. The building will take up twenty-five acres."

"I cannot fathom a building that big!"

"Some of the people living around here are fighting it. They feel the neighborhood would be changed because of noise and traffic. The market plans to bring two 20,000 gallon diesel-fuel storage tanks to the site."

"What an almighty scheme! It is hard for me to comprehend."

"Dad says we can attend town meetings to find out more and not to give up hope."

"He's right, my lad. I recall the Psalm, 'We will not fear, though the earth should change.' Let us remember that."

"There's some good news too. I found a box in the girls' bedroom fireplace. It had an abolitionist button in it. Dad says it proves the house was a station on the Underground Railroad."

"By golden, it was! The fugitives hid in the basement tunnel for safety."

"Did many hide there?"

"Ay-yup, sometimes a whole family. We sheltered and fed them during the day, so they could travel at night to freedom."

"I'm going to poke around and see if I can find anything else."

"Good, I would not be surprised if my daughter Vilera concealed more things."

"I can't stay long today. Dad wants to leave soon."

"All right, Joseph, I will absquatulate."

I scratched my head. "Ab–what?"

"Absquatulate—means to disappear, my lad."

He faded away.

But the Supermart building trouble stayed.

The evening paper had an article on the proposed supermarket building.

Dad cut it out. "Let's start collecting these. There's bound to be more and it will be easier to monitor progress."

I picked up the paper and read, "Supermart Picks Lancaster for Warehouse, $60 Million Distribution Center Will Employ 600."

"Dad, this says that the Town Supervisor is happy about the project."

"Sure, Joe. It would mean more taxes for the town. However, he also states he expects to hear from concerned residents. The Town Board and the Planning Board are having a joint meeting Wednesday night. Would you like to go with me?"

"You bet I would!"

———— ❈ ————

I fingered my baseball cap nervously at the meeting. We learned that town officials required an environmental impact statement from Supermart people. They had to file the statement soon. Then there would be a thirty-day comment period for both the public and government agencies to answer.

I pictured the house entangled in a giant web. My imagination let me smear whiteout over the tangle to free the house.

"It all sounds so complicated, Dad."

"It surely is, son. I'm afraid only time will tell the outcome."

I wondered how I could help. Maybe I'd think of something in school tomorrow.

CHAPTER 11

M r. Weston said, "Kids, we have lots to talk about. Supermart warehouse plans may affect Hull House as well as our whole community."

Richie wiggled. "I wonder if 'Brainiac' Joey can solve this mess!"

I raised my hand to share what I learned at the town meeting.

The teacher nodded his head. "I'm sure there will be lots of news on radio, TV, and in the papers."

Almost weekly, local newspapers featured a story on the project. Mr. Weston kept a log of headlines on a large chart in the classroom:

"Women Giving Out Fliers Ejected from Senior
    Citizens' Center; Literature opposes proposed
    Supermart distribution center in Lancaster"

"Hearing on Supermart Rezoning Bid Draws 100;
    Residents bombard Lancaster & company
    officials with questions"

"Supermart Project Enlivens Lancaster Forum;
    Hearing on comprehensive plan focuses
    on zoning"

"Supermart, Foes Square Off in Lancaster;
    Debate on warehouse not always friendly"

Mr. Weston said, "Before we discuss these headlines, I've got a brain teaser for you. Why did the man keep a ruler on his newspaper?"

No one answered.

"Give up? Because he wanted to get the story straight."

I thought, ugh, he should team up with my Dad and his riddles.

Mr. Weston walked over to the chart. "Okay, let's try to get *this* story straight. Think about the trailer trucks they will use. Each day, 319 trucks will enter and exit. That totals 638 trips daily, adding massive traffic."

Mike raised his hand. "We drive there a lot and my dad gets aggravated. He says they need a signal light."

"He's right, it's already a busy road," said Mr. Weston.

Next the teacher talked about the two unions that represented Supermart employees. They supported the project.

Richie said, "Yeah, my uncle works at Supermart and he's been going to meetings."

"Yes, Richie, many people are concerned about jobs," Mr. Weston replied. "We'll have to wait for the Town Board's vote."

My hopes were with the people opposing the building. The question "Could they win?" kept floating around in my brain. *I edited a scoreboard — Citizens 100, Supermart 0.*

The list of headlines on the chart grew:

"Western New York Can't Afford to Lose Jobs"

"Blatant Errors Alleged in Supermart Study on
Lancaster Facility; Opera House meeting
packed"

"Jobs Vie with Quality of Life in Lancaster as
Residents Split Over Supermart Warehouse"

Mr. Weston explained there were two sides to the story. One side now called itself CARE (Concerned Area Residents' Efforts). This group brought in an engineering professor. He argued that storm water running off the property would be carrying pollutants from truck exhaust. He also claimed that discharge from trucks and other sources was more than estimated in Supermart's statement.

The teacher frowned. "This is an important factor, class. What's going to happen to air and soil quality?"

On the other side, Supermart's attorney accused CARE of confusing the issue. He said if all these problems were not resolved to the satisfaction of the DEC (Department of Energy and Conservation), they would never get the permit to operate.

Mr. Weston said, "Remember, they will need a permit from DEC before they can build."

"Maybe they won't get the permit," said Ted.

Mr. Weston continued. "The Supermart organization is trying hard to make their proposal user friendly. They plan to set the warehouse back 1,000 feet from the road and 2,000 feet from the nearest home."

He wrote the figures on the blackboard. "Let's see. That's about three football fields from the road and about six fields from houses."

"I'll bet I could throw a football that far," bragged Richie.

Kids answered, "Yeah, sure Richie, fat chance, knock it off!"

The teacher said, "Next, think about air pollution. The huge trucks will generate about 1,400 – 3,600 pounds of carbon monoxide annually. This is apparently within legal limits, but it sounds like a lot, doesn't it?"

Brucie said, "Sure does! I'd probably have to hold my nose all the time."

"You wouldn't have to, Bruce. Carbon monoxide is a colorless, odorless, but highly poisonous gas. The legal limits count on it dissipating into the air without harm," said Mr. Weston.

My video eye saw the class walking around with gas masks on their faces. Not a pretty sight!

Mr. Weston looked thoughtfully at the class. "Supermart plans a nature preserve for the southern portion of the land. Will this make up for the traffic and pollution problems?"

The class seemed as divided as the community. But everyone worried about how it would affect Hull House.

During two visits to the house, I read parts of the articles to the ghost. Sometimes his voice would quiver in agitation, saying "Sakes Alive!" or he would drone, "Do not comprehend."

Then I told him about all the neighbors putting big "SUPERMART NO" signs in front of their houses on Genesee Street.

He said, "Maybe they will prevail."

In my heart I knew that the problem seemed to be growing, looming as large as the distribution center itself.

One Sunday, I searched around the fireplace again. I was about to give up when a brick felt loose at the bottom.

I picked up a thin piece of wood from the floor and wedged it underneath. It released the brick and revealed another box. This one was metal and larger than the first one. But it had the same initials—VH.

I called down to the kitchen where my father was working.

"Dad, come on up. I found something!"

He ran in. "You're becoming quite a detective, Joey. What do you have here?"

We sat on the floor and I handed him the box. It was old and rusty. Dad had to wrestle with it a few minutes. Finally, the cover popped. Inside were tiny scissors, corroded and bumpy with rust. Underneath them were pieces of colored cloth.

"It looks like sewing stuff, Dad."

"You're right. These small squares were probably for a quilt. Look at this little booklet. It holds needles."

I turned it over and saw the words, 'May the point of our needles prick the slave owner's conscience.'

"This must have been part of Vilera's abolitionist movement."

"Yes, Joe. Women's antislavery societies made piecework quilts. The first antislavery fair took place in Boston in 1834. They sold quilts and other things to raise money for the cause."

"Maybe Vilera went there!"

"Maybe, though we'll never know for sure. This box is more strong proof that Hull House was a station for runaway slaves."

He grabbed my hand and shook it. "Good work, Joey!"

I wanted to tell him that I'd know for sure about Vilera soon, after I talked to Warren Hull.

CHAPTER 12

Dad got another important phone call Monday. He hung up, shaking his head.

"Guess what, Joey? The Supermart project has developed a new wrinkle! It's an even deeper one."

"What, Dad, what?"

"They found an Indian village buried at the warehouse site. Supermart has hired an archeological firm to continue the excavation. They will need permission from the state to use the site of the Indian remains for their project."

I jumped up from my seat and shouted, "Wow, Dad, that is big news!"

"It's one of the most important sites in Western New York, one of the few known Iroquois villages with a large amount of recoverable artifacts."

"Will this new development help save the area?"

"I don't know, Joey, we'll have to wait and see."

A week later, Dad brought me up to date. "The archeologists working with Supermart have located remains of a small Indian village. It dates from about 1300 to 1350, the late Woodland period. The future of the site is linked to the Supermart project."

I frowned. "I don't understand. How, Dad?"

"Well, there are state historic guidelines governing

such sites. If the Town Board should approve Supermart's proposal, the company would have to pay for the digging and removal of artifacts from the site."

"Maybe they'll decide to build somewhere else."

"That would not help the native American ruins because the source of funding for the excavation would be lost. It's a real dilemma."

"Man, I thought Hull House was old. The Indian site is almost five hundred years older!"

"Yes, it's another important piece of our history."

"Would Supermart have to wait to build until the archeologists finish there?"

"No, they have agreed to work around the site, so both projects could proceed simultaneously. The Town Board is still waiting for the final environmental report."

I paced up and down the room, shaking my head.

"This waiting is for the birds!"

"I know, son. What helps me is to think of a Proverb, 'Commit your work to the Lord, and your plans will be established.' It boosts my trust that the right decision will be made."

Where had I heard those words before?

"Dad, you really like proverbs, don't you?"

"Sure, Joe, I think they're like little sound bytes, chips of knowledge that provide an insight to life. Sometimes they can give us the strength to deal with problems as they come along."

My memory flashed back to the ghost. "I guess lots of people like to quote them."

Dad smiled. "They can help us to understand the high and low notes in the melody of life."

That evening as I was brushing my dog, I whispered in her floppy ear.

"Gosh Libby, there doesn't seem to be an easy answer to this whole problem. Trying to help the ghost is getting harder and more complicated. If the Supermart building is not approved, the Indian site is in danger. If they do build, it could mean trouble for Hull House. Dad says maybe there will be a solution to preserve both. I hope so, old girl."

Libby swished against my legs in a dog hug and whimpered her sympathy.

⊷⊶ ⧓ ⊷⊶

I was itching to tell the ghost the two latest happenings. When I told him about the Indian village, he quivered.

"Sakes alive, Joseph. I know just where they are digging. It used to be part of my cousin's land!"

"Wow! How did you know it was an Indian site?"

"One of his Seneca friends told him it was sacred ground and pleaded with him not to farm in that area. The Indian was so earnest, my cousin agreed not to disturb the ground. In gratitude, the tribe gave him an Indian name 'Hodanidoah.' It meant 'merciful man.'"

"Neat!"

"I recall the tract was located 150 paces north of a huge elm tree."

I said, "Now the state will allow digging and wants to preserve all the objects found there."

"Land sakes, Joseph, all creation seems to be getting involved. Where will it all end?"

"I don't know, but the Board meeting is in two days."

"Then we will know soon."

"Yeah, soon."

"Remember to keep the faith, lad."

"I will. My good news is that I found another treasure. I checked out the fireplace again in the girls' bedroom."

I described the sewing box and Dad's explanation of the quilts.

"By golden, I recall Vilera journeying to Boston around 1834 with a group of women. Polly and I were very worried about the trip, but our daughter was determined."

"Then she must have attended the first women's abolitionist fair."

"Ay-yup, that was its name, lad."

"Awesome. It's all fitting together, like a puzzle. I sure hope we don't lose any of the pieces after the vote."

That night, in bed, I got an idea. What if I went to see where the archeologists were digging? Maybe I could find that big elm tree and measure off 150 paces. I know Warren Hull's feet would have been bigger than mine, but I could make giant steps. The major problem was there were No Trespassing signs there. Also, Dad didn't allow me to ride my bike on Genesee Street with all that traffic.

Before I fell asleep, I edited my bike to have wings and the power to fly me wherever I wanted to go.

CHAPTER 13

I could hardly eat dinner on the night of the Board meeting. The butterflies in my stomach flew up to my brain and back.

Dad was as eager as I was to get there.

The meeting was held in the Lancaster Opera House. It was packed with 350 people. Everyone waited to hear the five Council members cast their vote.

My heart pounded as loudly as the gavel calling the meeting to order. *My camera eye put big, black robes and white, curly judge's wigs on those five guys.*

Debate lasted only thirty minutes. The final count was four to one to rezone 85 acres of farmland for the warehouse! Board members said the town would gain more taxes and jobs would be created.

After the vote, the room was quiet. Some people saying "Oh, no!" broke the silence. Others clapped and cheered.

I sighed. "It's not fair! It's a rip-off!"

I edited and put dunce caps on the voters and sat them in the corner.

My father winked and patted my hand. "It'll be okay, son."

The Board approved a statement listing things Supermart would do to help the community.

They would install a traffic signal at the entrance to the warehouse. Landscaping would screen the building. They would provide equipment for the Bowmansville Fire Department. They would also pay for the archeological dig of the Indian village.

When I heard the last part, I thought, good. At least that would save the Indian relics.

Later, I asked Dad what he thought about the decision.

"I guess I'm not surprised, Joe. I sometimes think it was a done deal from the start. We must accept the resolution and find a way to work with it."

"Do you think Hull House will be safe?"

"So far, so good. I understand the street widening will be on the other side of Genesee. I'm still searching for funds, but I've had several offers from people wanting to help with the restoration."

"Did finding Vilera's boxes help?"

"Immensely, Joey. They have great historical importance. They add to the value of Hull House."

"Maybe there's more hidden somewhere."

"Maybe, keep looking. It helps to keep the house in the public eye in a positive frame."

"Are you still planning to offer tours?"

"Yes, several groups have shown interest. The next step is to train guides called docents. I think the house will be fine, just fine."

◄ ━ ⊠ ━ ►

Waiting three days to see the ghost seemed as long as the week before Christmas. I was jumpy until I finally stroked the glass in the attic.

"Welcome, Joseph."

"I have the answer from the Board meeting."

His image was very still. "I am prepared to hear, lad."

He hummed when I finished.

I tried to sound more cheerful. "Dad's pretty sure the house will be safe."

He quivered. "Praise the Lord!"

"We still need money, but Dad is searching for grants. He plans to start repairs with volunteers."

"By golden, that is a good sign. Seems all has been done that can be for now."

"When school ends, I plan on working here too. Dad says there's lots of ways I can help, like sanding woodwork and cleaning up."

"My dear lad, you should stand tall. You have already done a whopping job, and I am proud of you. Thank you for all your help."

I shuffled my feet on the dusty floor and cleared my throat.

"You're not going to leave forever, are you?"

"Not quite yet, my lad. I would like to observe the repair work. But it will be more difficult to communicate with so many workers around."

"Yeah, I probably won't be alone much. Maybe I'll be able to sneak up sometime."

"If you need to communicate with me, please return and I shall try to answer. Remember you have my profound gratitude. Farewell, Joseph."

As the ghost vanished, I stared at the window for a minute. It seemed his presence lingered, like smoke from a campfire. I waved good-bye, turned and ran down the stairs, already missing him.

CHAPTER 14

All summer, volunteers worked at Hull House with pounding hammers and screaming saws. A cabinet maker refinished the peeling front door and repaired woodwork in the boys' bedroom. In the girls' bedroom, carpenters built a new fireplace frame. Dad bought a large mantle at an auction to replace the missing one in the kitchen.

To get the house back to its original 1810 condition, they had to get rid of some stuff. Plumbers pulled out showers and sinks installed in the 1930's; electricians worked on wiring; masons repaired the decaying chimney; people scraped and sanded walls and woodwork. My father directed and worked right along with the volunteers.

I helped him lug trash and do errands. I used my camera to record the changes and added to my scrapbook. The only thing missing was a picture of the ghost. I kept thinking how happy he must be to see the house taking shape.

As one repair led to another, I could see the results. It was like skimming a pebble in a pond and watching the ripples it made.

I kept looking for hidden objects. There were no more loose bricks in any of the rooms.

My curiosity led me to search down in the cellar, near the tunnel area the ghost mentioned. I poked along the open beams with a yardstick. Dad and I were both there when I hit something stuck up in a rafter. A soft object fell into my hands.

"Whoa! Look, Dad. It seems to be a bag of some kind."

"Handle it carefully, Joe. Put it on the work bench so we can examine it."

The fabric was very dusty and full of holes. It was shaped like a pouch and had a drawstring handle.

"Dad, this looks like a lady's reticule! Remember the ones sold at the open house?"

"Yes, sure looks like one."

I gently opened the fragile-looking purse. Inside I found paper money, but it was all torn up into pieces.

"Looks like someone was hiding money," I said.

"Right, but I think mice have chewed through and destroyed the bills. They may have made a nest here."

"I wonder if Vilera hid this bag too."

Dad said, "Or it could have been someone on the Underground Railroad. Maybe she had to leave quickly and forgot to retrieve it."

Goosebumps crawled across my skin. I pictured a girl like Monica. She had to be scared, running for her life. *My version of this scene would be to block the slave hunters, big time. I'd bring back the wild panthers to catch them.*

I said, "What a creepy idea that it might have belonged to a girl, hiding herself."

I turned the bag over. "It looks so old, Dad."

He said, "It could have been left here 150 years ago. Let's spread everything out at home and see if we can piece the bills together. It might give us a clue to a date."

"Let's see if anything else is up there." I moved the yardstick across the entire beam, felt something solid, swept it down and it fell with a plunk. I bent and picked it up.

"Look, Dad, it's a shoe, a woman's shoe!" It felt heavy in my hands.

Dad touched it and said, "Amazing! Looks as if the mice had lunch on the fabric high-top. Some of the small buttons are missing, but the design is still fairly clear. The wooden heel is about 3 inches. See how the thick wooden sole is attached with tiny nails? The shoemaker was quite a craftsman. Wasn't there a mate up there?"

"No, I've rechecked. Why do you suppose there's only one?"

"We can only guess, Joey. Maybe the hiding girl did not have time to recover it before fleeing."

"I wonder how old it is?"

Dad said, "We should take it to the Amherst Museum. Perhaps they can help us date it."

I turned it over in my hand. "I have so many questions. Who wore it? How old was she? Where did she walk? Gosh Dad, it's like history is coming alive in this house!"

He rubbed his hand over my head. "It seems you're as hooked on Hull House history as I am. Glad to have you aboard, Joey. You're a big help. This tangible evidence may help in our grant applications."

━━ ▆◆▆ ━━

One day in July, Dad received a fantastic letter. It was from a local foundation awarding a grant of $125,000 for Hull House restoration.

My father read the letter out loud and ended with a happy "Yes!" He grabbed my hands and swung me around.

"Yahoo," I yelled.

Libby started barking. She snapped up the envelope Dad had dropped and began prancing like a pony. Back and forth she trotted, holding her head high, as if she won a prize. She made a funny sound like "yay, yay, yay." Her tail swished and fluttered like a flag. This was her show-off pose. She wanted us to know she was as happy as we were!

Dad said, "Seems this good news brought joy to all of us, even your dog. It will also be welcomed by the spirit of Hull House."

I stared at him goggle-eyed. He winked at me. What did spirit mean? Did he mean the ghost? Did he know about him? Naw, it couldn't be, could it?

Dad said, "Get in the car, Joey. We're going to Hull House."

I followed him in a daze.

When he started the car, I asked, "What did you mean by the spirit of Hull House?"

He grinned. "I guess it's confession time, Joe. I saw the Ghost of Warren Hull in the attic too. I was just about your age when my dad took me there."

I gasped. "Why didn't you tell me this before, Dad?"

"I wanted you to enjoy your secret friend, just like I did. Also, I hoped you would use your own ideas to help save the house, and you did."

"Gosh, Dad, this is a real surprise!"

"I know, Joey. Now that we're here, I figure you want to tell the ghost about the letter."

"You bet I do!"

I hurried to the attic and rubbed the glass anxiously. It seemed a long time before the ghost answered.

"Ahh, Joseph."

"I hoped I could reach you after all this time. I have some super news!"

I could hardly keep from jumping up and down as I told about the grant.

His voice boomed, "Hallelujah, that is the best news yet!"

I asked, "Have you seen how much work has been done on your house?"

"Ay-yup. I have witnessed a great spirit of cooperation in all the workers. However, you are still the biggest toad in the puddle."

"What does that mean?"

"It means you are the most important one in the group. Your father could not have advanced this far without your contributions."

I said, "Dad told me today that he knows you too."

"By golden, I have been hoping he would tell you."

"Now I know why my father worked so hard. You really wanted me to help him, didn't you?"

The ghost's face beamed with a satisfied smile.

He said, "My observations told me that you truly comprehended what needed to be done and were willing to work. I am reminded of the Proverb, 'By wisdom a house is built, and by understanding it is established.' Your help has made the re-establishment of my house possible. I am much obliged to you. Now.........we must part."

I didn't want him to go. *The sadness I felt made me wish I could reach through the window and touch the ghost.*

"Will I be able to visit you in the future?"

"You may try, just as you did today. But I am weary and look forward to my rest. I am finally content that my house is safe. Farewell, farewell, farewell my dear boy."

I waved as his image faded. I turned, slunk down the stairs, and left with a lonely lump in my throat. I couldn't swallow it away for many weeks, no matter how hard I tried.

AUTHOR'S NOTES

Joey's story is set in the existing Hull House in Lancaster, New York. It is listed on the National Register of Historic Places. Revolutionary War veteran Warren Hull (1762-1838) built the stone dwelling in 1810. Preservationists are working hard toward their goal of restoring and using it for a museum.

I am grateful to John Conlin, former Director of the Landmark Society of the Niagara Frontier, for sharing his knowledge of the real Hull House. His passion for preservation was evident as he spoke of Warren Hull, his home and his family. In one of our many conversations, John related how he took his eight-year-old grandson to visit Hull House. As they approached the attic, the boy asked, "Grandpa, is there a ghost here?" Of course he was assured that ghosts do not exist, but many people have noticed an aura in the house that is out-of-the-ordinary.

Joey's encounters in Hull House were inspired by research of the time period. Some dates have been changed to enhance the story. The names of the Hull family members are authentic. Vilera Hull, youngest of the twelve children, died in 1835. Her gravestone is the last surviving upright stone in the family cemetery behind Hull House.

Underground Railroad:

The noted preservationist, Austin M. Fox, wrote of Hull House as a station on the Underground Railroad in "The Train Into Canada." This secretive system arose when escaped slaves sought refuge. In addition to the many people that harbored fugitive slaves in their homes, others indirectly aided them by donating money or clothing. They also attended lectures and paid a fee to help the cause. Some citizens became informants for the "conductors," warning about an imminent raid on a safe-house. Through the compassion and generosity of these people, many of the escaped slaves eventually made their way to freedom in Canada.

Sometimes, runners with fast horses carried the fugitives from one station to the next. Utmost secrecy had to be observed since the consequences for assisting a runaway were costly. In the Compromise of 1850, the Fugitive Slave Law imposed a fine of $1,000 and imprisonment of up to six months.

Another danger was that of bounty hunters crossing into Canada to capture the runaways, returning them to their "masters" to collect a legal bounty and a reward. There is little documentation about the Underground Railroad because people did not want to leave clues to implicate them in this illegal humanitarian endeavor.

Abolitionist Movement:

A photo of the Abolitionist Button is shown in *The Waking Dream*. This catalog accompanied The Metropolitan Museum Of Art's exhibition in 1993 on Photography's First Century. The miniature daguerreotype (⅜ in.) shows two hands clasped together, one white, one black, resting on a Bible. The photo is held by a two-piece, gold-washed brass frame. A loop on the reverse is for sewing onto clothing. The simple case design is typical of metal buttons mass-produced in New England factories from 1830 to 1850. This button was discovered in a Massachusetts flea market in the early 1980s.

It is stored at the Metropolitan Museum of Art and may be viewed only by appointment. I was awe-struck when I saw the button. Its powerful message belies its tiny size. The button, as well as piecework quilts made by women's antislavery societies, may have been made to raise money for the abolitionist cause. Women organized antislavery fairs, accepting "all well-made, useful, and ornamental products." Boston was the center of the abolitionist movement and was the site of the first fair in 1834. The creators of the fair preferred articles incorporating political texts, such as a needlebook inscribed "May the point of our needles prick the slave owner's conscience."

Reticules:

In the early 1800s, ladies' fashions changed to a narrow silhouette with no room for bulging pockets. This led to the creation of reticules, bags gathered at the top with drawstring handles. They were also called "indispensables."

The French mocked them by the term "ridicules" which led to the final name—reticules. Fashionable ladies in Europe had elaborate bags made of satin, velvet or silk, ornately decorated with beads, bangles or sequins.

Of course, early pioneers made their own clothing as well as homemade varieties of handbags. Leather types became popular as early as 1820 when shops selling dry goods specialized in leather reticules.

<u>Psalm 23, The Bible:</u>

"The Lord is my shepherd; I shall not want.

He maketh me to lie down in green pastures:

He leadeth me beside the still waters.

He restoreth my soul:

He leadeth me in the paths of righteousness

For His name's sake.

Yea, though I walk through the valley

Of the shadow of death, I will fear no evil:

for thou art with me;

thy rod and thy staff they comfort me

Thou preparest a table before me

in the presence of mine enemies:

thou annointest my head with oil;

my cup runneth over.

Surely goodness and mercy shall follow me

all the days of my life:

and I will dwell in the house of the Lord forever."

As a guest lecturer at the Chautauqua Institute on August 13, 1996, Patricia Locke related the Native American version of Psalm 23. She is a MacArthur

Fellow and member of the Lakota and Chippewa tribes. She said this interpretation was favored by Native tribes because "it made them understand the Black Robes (Christian missionaries) were human beings too," understanding God the same way. Her talk emphasized that people everywhere are related and all need love, joy and understanding.

SELECTED BIBLIOGRAPHY

Aiken, John; Wilhelms, John; Brunger, Eric; and Aiken, Richard. <u>Outpost of Empires</u>. Phoenix: Frank E. Richards, 1961.

Bissell, Eleanor. "Early Town History of the Town of Lancaster." Lancaster, 1953-54. (Mimeographed.)

Blaney, Robert Earl. <u>150 Years</u>. Being the History of the Presbyterian Society of Cayuga Creek. Lancaster: Lancaster Enterprise, 1968.

Conlin, John H., Former Director, Landmark Society of the Niagara Frontier. Interviews 1992-2001.

Conlin, John H. "The Warren Hull House." <u>Buffalo Spree</u>, Spring 1998, p. 50-52.

Ettinger, Roseann. <u>Handbags</u>. West Chester: Schiffer Publishing, Ltd., 1991.

Fox, Austin M. "The Train Into Canada." <u>Buffalo Spree</u>, Winter 1995, pp. 44-45.

Greenwood, Barbara. <u>A Pioneer Sampler</u>. New York: Ticknor & Fields, 1995.

Hambourg, Maria Morris; Apraxine, Pierre; Daniel, Malcolm; Rosenheim, Jeff L.; and Heckert, Virginia. <u>The Waking Dream</u>. New York: The Metropolitan Museum of Art, Distributed by Harry N. Abrams, Inc., 1993.

Laycock, George and Ellen Laycock. <u>How the Settlers Lived</u>. New York: David McKay Co., Inc., 1980.

Lindberg, Olga. <u>Family Life in Early Buffalo</u>. Adventures in Western New York History, Vol. XXIII. Buffalo: Buffalo and Erie County Historical Society, 1975.

Locke, Patricia. "A Version of Psalm 23." <u>The Chautauquan Daily</u>, 14 August 1996, p. 3.

Sterling, Dorothy. <u>Lucretia Mott, Gentle Warrior</u>. Garden City: Doubleday & Co., Inc., 1964.

Tunis, Edward. <u>The Young United States: 1783-1830</u>. New York: The World Pub. Co., 1969.

Turner, O. <u>Pioneer History of the Holland Purchase</u>. Geneseo: James Brunner, 1974.

Yates, Raymond F. <u>Under Three Flags</u>. Buffalo: Henry Stewart, Inc., 1958.